George Manville Fenn

By Birth a Lady

A tale. Vol. 1

George Manville Fenn

By Birth a Lady
A tale. Vol. 1

ISBN/EAN: 9783337344276

Printed in Europe, USA, Canada, Australia, Japan

Cover: Foto ©Andreas Hilbeck / pixelio.de

More available books at **www.hansebooks.com**

BY BIRTH A LADY.

LONDON:
RODSON AND SONS, PRINTERS, PANCRAS ROAD, N.W.

BY BIRTH A LADY.

A Tale.

BY

GEORGE MANVILLE FENN,

AUTHOR OF 'MAD,' 'WEBS IN THE WAY,' ETC.

IN THREE VOLUMES.

VOL. I.

LONDON:

TINSLEY BROTHERS, 18 CATHERINE ST., STRAND

1871.

CONTENTS OF VOL. I.

BY BIRTH A LADY.

CHAPTER I.

SOMETHING ABOUT A LETTER.

'He mustn't have so much corn, Joseph,' said Mr. Tiddson, parish doctor of Croppley Magna, addressing a grinning boy of sixteen, who, with his smock-frock rolled up and twisted round his waist, was holding the bridle of a very thin, dejected-looking pony, whose mane and tail seemed to have gone to the cushion-maker's, leaving in their places a few strands that had missed the shears. The pony's eyes were half shut, and his nose hung low; but, as if attending to his master's words, one ear was twitched back, while the other pointed forward; and no sooner had his owner finished speaking than the poor little beast whinnied softly and shook its evidently remonstrating head. 'He mustn't have so much corn, Joseph,' said Mr. Tiddson importantly. 'He's growing wild and vicious, and it was as much as I could do this morning to hold him.'

'What did he do, zir?' said the boy, grinning a wider grin.

'Do, Joseph? He wanted to go after the hounds, and took the bit in his teeth, and kicked when they crossed the road. I shall have to diet him. Give him some water, Joseph, but no corn.'

The poor pony might well shake his head, for it was a standing joke in Croppley that the doctor tried experiments on that pony: feeding him with chaff kept in an oaty bag, and keeping him low and greyhound-like of rib, for the sake of speed when a union patient was ill.

But the pony had to be fetched out again before Joseph had removed his saddle; for just as Mr. Tiddson was taking off his gloves and overcoat, a man came running up to the door, and tore at the bell, panting the while with his exertions.

'Well, what now? Is Betty Starger worse?'

'No,'—puff—'no, sir;'—puff—'it's—it's—'

'Well? Why don't you speak, man?'

'Breath, sir!'—puff. 'Run—all way!'—puff.

'Yes, yes,' said Mr. Tiddson. 'And now what is it?'

'Hax—haxiden, sir,' puffed the messenger.

'Bless my soul, my good man! Where?' exclaimed the doctor, rubbing his hands.

'Down by Crossroads, sir; and they war takin' a gate off the hinges to lay him on, and carry him to the Seven Bells, when I run for you, sir.'

'And how was it?—and who is it?' said the doctor.

'Gent, sir; along o' the hounds.'

'Here, stop a minute,' exclaimed the doctor, ringing furiously till a servant came. 'Jane, tell Joseph to bring Peter round directly; I'm wanted.—Now go on, my good man,' he continued.

'See him comin' myself, sir. Dogs had gone over the fallows, givin' mouth bea-u-u-tiful, when he comes — this gent, you know—full tear, lifts his horse, clears the hedge, and drops into the lane—Rugley-lane, you know, sir, where the cutting is, with the sand-martins' nestes in the bank. Well, sir, he comes down nice as could be, and then put his horse at t'other bank, as it couldn't be expected to get up, though it did try; and then, before you know'd it, down it come back'ards, right on to the poor gent, and rolled over him, so that when three or four on us got up he was as white and still as your 'ankychy, sir, that he war; and so I come off arter you. And you ain't got sech a thing as a drop o' beer in the house, have you, sir?'

'No, my man, I have not,' said Mr. Tiddson, mounting his steed, which had just been brought round to the front; 'but if you will call at my surgery when I return, I daresay I can find you a glass of something.—Go on, Peter.'

But Peter did not seem disposed to go on; and it was not until his bare ribs had been drummed by the doctor's heels, and he had been smitten between the ears by the doctor's umbrella, that he condescended to shuffle off in a shambling trot—a pace that put the messenger to no inconvenience to keep alongside, since it was only about half the rate at which he had brought the news.

To have seen Mr., or, as he was generally called, *Dr.* Tiddson ride, any one would have called to mind the printed form upon his medicine labels—'To be well shaken;' for he was well shaken in the process, and had at short intervals to push forward his hat, which made a point of getting down over his ears. But, though not effectively, Dr. Tiddson and his pony Peter managed to shuffle over the ground, and arrived at the Seven Bells—a little roadside inn—just as four labouring men bore a gate to the door, and then, carefully lifting an insensible figure, carried it into the parlour, where a mattress had been prepared by the landlady.

Dr. Tiddson did not have an accident to tend every day, while those he did have

to do with were the mishaps of very ordinary people. This, then, was something
to make him descend from his pony with
the greatest of dignity, throwing the reins
to the messenger, and entering the little
parlour as if monarch of all he surveyed.

'Tut—tut—tut!' he exclaimed. 'Clear
the room directly; the man wants air.
Mrs. Pottles, send every one out, and lock
that door.'

The sympathising landlady obeyed, and
then the examination commenced.

'Hum!' muttered the doctor. 'Ribs
crushed — two, four, certainly; probable
laceration of the right lobe; concussion of
the brain, evidently. And what have we
here? Dear me! A sad case, Mrs. Pottles;
a fracture of the clavicle, I fear.'

'Lawk a deary me! Poor gentleman!
he 'ave got it bad,' said the landlady, raising her hands.

'Yes, Mrs. Pottles,' said the doctor, compressing his lips, 'it is, I fear, a serious case. But we must do what we can, Mrs. Pottles—we must do what we can.'

'Of course we must, sir!' exclaimed the landlady. 'And what shall us do first?'

'Let me see; another pillow, I think, Mrs. Pottles,' said the doctor, not heeding the question. 'He will not be able to leave here for some time to come.'

Mrs. Pottles sighed; and then from time to time supplied the doctor with bandages, water, sponge, and such necessaries as he needed; when, the patient presenting an appearance of recovering from his swoon, they watched him attentively.

'He won't die this time, Mrs. Pottles,' said the doctor, with authority.

'Lawk a deary me! no, sir, I hope not,' said the landlady—'a fine, nice, handsome

young fellow like he! He'll live and break
some 'arts yet, I'll be bound. It's all
very well for old folks like us, sir, to die ;
but I shouldn't like to see him go that-a-
way—just when out taking his pleasure,
too.'

Mr. Tiddson did not consider himself
one of the 'old folks,' so did not reply.

'A poor dear!' said Mrs. Pottles. 'I
wonder who he is? There'll be more 'n
one pair o' bright eyes wet because of his'
misfortun', I know. You've no idee, sir,
how like he is to my Tom—him as got
into that bit of trouble with the squire, sir.'

'Pooh, woman!—not a bit. Tchsh!'

The raised finger of the doctor accompanied his ejaculation, as the patient un-
closed his eyes, muttered a little, and then,
turning his head, seemed to sink into a
state of half sleep, half stupor.

The doctor sat for some time before

speaking, frowning severely at the landlady, and then impatiently pulling down
the blind to get rid of half a dozen lads,
who were spoiling the symmetry of their
noses against the window.

'I s'pose you have no idea who he is?'
said the doctor at last.

'Not the leastest bit in the world, sir.
They do say they've had a tremenjus run
to-day. But perhaps we shall have some
of the gents coming back this way, and
they may know him.'

'Precisely so, Mrs. Pottles; but you'd
better feel in his pockets, and we may be
able to find out where his friends are, and
so send them word of his condition.'

'Lawk a deary me, sir! But wouldn't
it be wrong for me to be peeping and pok-
ing in his pockets? But how so be if *you*
wish it, sir, I'll look.'

'I *don't* wish it, Mrs. Pottles; but it is

our duty to acquaint his friends, so you had better search.'

Now Mrs. Pottles's fingers were itching to make an examination ; and doubtless, had the doctor left, her first act would have been to 'peep and poke,' as she termed it ; so, taking up garment after garment, she drew out a handsome gold watch and seal chain with an eagle crest ; then a cigar-case bearing the same crest, and the letters 'C. V.;' and lastly a plain porte-monnaie, containing four sovereigns and some silver.

'No information there, Mrs. Pottles. But I'll make a list of these, and leave them in your charge till the patient re-covers.'

'Lawk a deary me, no, sir, don't do that ! We're as honest as the day is long here, sir, so don't put no temptation in our way. Make a list of the gentleman, if you

like, and leave *him* in our charge, and we'll
nurse him well again ; but you'd better
take the watch and things along of you.'

'Very good, Mrs. Pottles—ve-ery good,'
said the doctor, noting down the articles
he placed in his pocket, and thinking that,
even if called upon for no further atten-
dance, through the coming of some family
doctor, he was safe of the amount in the
portemonnaie, for he considered that no
gentleman would dream of taking that
back.

'And you think he'll get well, then,
sir ?' said Mrs. Pottles.

'Ye-e-e-s—yes, with care, Mrs. Pottles
—with care. But I'll ride over to my surgery now, and obtain a little medicine. I
shall be back in an hour.'

Mrs. Pottles curtsied him out, and then
returned to seat herself by her injured visitor, looking with motherly admiration on

his broad white forehead and thick golden
beard, as she again compared him with her
Tom, who got into that bit of trouble with
the squire. But before the doctor had been
gone an hour, the patient began to display
sundry restless movements, ending by opening his eyes widely and fixing them upon
the landlady.

'Who are you? and where am I?' he
exclaimed. 'Let me see, though—I recollect now : my horse came down with me.
I don't think I'm much hurt, though.'

'O, but you are, sir, and very badly,
too. Mr. Tiddson says you are to be very
quiet.'

'Who the deuce is Mr. Tiddson?' said
the patient, trying to rise, but sinking back
with a groan.

'Lawk a deary me, sir! I thought everybody know'd Mr. Tiddson : he's our doctor,
and they do say as he's very clever ; but

he ain't in rheumatiz, for he never did me a bit o' good.'

'Poor dad!' muttered the young man thoughtfully, and then aloud: 'Give me a pen and ink and a sheet of paper.'

'But sewer*ly*, sir, you're not going to try to—'

'Get me the pen and ink, woman!' exclaimed the sufferer impatiently.

Mrs. Pottles raised her hands, and then hurriedly placed a little dirty blotting-case before her guest, holding it and the rusty ink so that he was able to write a short note, which he signed, and then doubled hastily, for he was evidently in pain.

'Let some man take that to the King's Arms at Lexville, and ask for Mr. Bray. If he is not there, let them send for him; but the note is to be given to no one else.'

'Very good, sir,' said the woman; 'but it's a many miles there. How's he to go?'

'Ride—ride!' exclaimed the sufferer impatiently, and then he sank back deeper in his pillow.

'I didn't think, or I would have sent for some one else,' he muttered, after a pause; 'but I daresay he will come.'

And then he lay thinking in a dreamy, semi-delirious fashion of the contents of that note—a note so short, and yet of itself containing matter that might bring to the writer a life of regret, and to another, loving, gentle, and true-hearted, the breaking of that true gentle heart, and the cold embrace of the bridegroom Death!

CHAPTER II.

' BAI JOVE !'

THREE months after the incidents recorded
in the last chapter, Littleborough Station,
on the Great Middleland and Conjunction
Railway, woke into life; for it was nearly
noon, and the mid-day up-train would soon
run alongside of the platform, stay for the
space of half a minute, and then proceed
again on its hurrying, panting course towards the great metropolis; for though
such a thing did sometimes happen, the
taking up or setting down of passengers at
Littleborough was not as a matter of course.
Nobody ever wanted to come to Littleborough, which was three miles from the
station, and very few people ever seemed

to take tickets from Littleborough to proceed elsewhere: the consequence being that
the station-master—a fair young man with
budding whiskers, and a little cotton-woolly
moustache—spent the greater part of his
time in teaching a rough dog to stand upon
his hind-legs, to walk, beg, smoke pipes,
and perform various other highly interest-
ing feats, while the one porter spent his in
yawning and playing 'push halfpenny,' right
hand against left—a species of gambling
that left him neither richer nor poorer at
the day's end. But his yawning was something frightful, being extensive enough to
have startled a child into the belief that
ogres really had an existence in the flesh,
though the said porter was after all but a
simple, lazy, ignorant boor, with as little of
harm in his nature as there was of activity.

But, as before said, Littleborough Station now woke into life; for after crawling

into the booking-office, and yawning fright-
fully at the clock, the porter went and
turned a handle, altering the position of a
signal, and then returned to find the station-master framed in the little doorway
through which he issued tickets, and now
pitching little bits of biscuit for the dog
to catch.

'Here's summun a-coming!' said the
porter, excitedly running to the door and
checking a yawn half-way.

'No!—is there?' cried the station-master, running out, catching up the dog and
carrying it in, to shut himself up once
more behind his official screen and railway-
clerk dignity.

'Swell in a dog-cart, with groom a-
drivin',' said the porter aloud; and then,
as the vehicle came nearer: 'Portmanty
and bag with him, and that there gum's all
dried up, and won't stick on no labels.

Blest if here ain't somebody else, too, in the
'Borough fly, and two boxes on the top.'

The porter threw open the doors very
widely, the station-master tried his ticket-
stamper to see if it would work, and then
peered excitedly out for the coming tra-
vellers.

He had not to wait long. The smart
dog-cart was drawn up at the door; and as
the horse stood champing its bit and throwing the white foam in all directions, a very
languid, carefully-dressed gentleman descended, waved his hand towards his luggage and wrappers in answer to the porter's
obsequious salute, and then sauntering,
cigar in hand, to the station-master's
pigeon-hole, he languidly drawled out:

'First cla-a-ass—London.'

'Twenty-eight-and-six, sir,' said the
station-master, when the traveller slowly
placed a sovereign and a half before him.

'Tha-a-anks. No! Give the change to the porter fellare.' And the new arrival strolled on to the platform, leaving the porter grinning furiously, and carrying the portmanteau and bag about without there being the slightest necessity for such proceedings.

Meanwhile the fly had drawn up, the driver dismounted, and opened the door for a closely veiled young lady in black to alight, when she proceeded to pay the man.

'Suthin' for the driver, miss, please,' said the fellow gruffly.

'I understood from your master that the charge would be five shillings to the station,' said the new arrival, in a low tremulous voice.

'Yes, miss, but the driver's allus hextry. Harf-crown most people gives the driver.'

There was no sound issued from beneath that veil, but the motion of the dress

showed that something very much like a
sigh must have been struggling for exit as
a little soft white hand drew a florin from
a scantily-furnished purse, and gave it to
the man.

'Humph,' growled the fellow, 'things
gets wuss and wuss;' and climbing on to
his box - seat, he gathered up reins and
whip, and sat stolid and surly without
moving.

'Will you be kind enough to lift down
my trunks?' said the traveller gently.

'You must ast the porter for that 'ere,'
said the man: 'we're drivers, we are, and
'tain't our business.   Here, Joe, come and
get these here trunks off the roof;' and he
accompanied his words with a meaning
wink to the porter, which gentleman, in
the full possession of an unlooked - for
eighteenpence, felt so wealthy that he could
afford to be supercilious.

'What class, miss?' he said, reaching his hand to a trunk.

'Third, if you please,' was the reply.

'Ah! there'll be something extry to pay for luggidge: third-class passengers ain't allowed two big boxes like these here. —Why didn't you put 'em down, Dick?'

'Ain't got half paid for what I did do,' said the driver gruffly. 'People as can't afford to pay for flies oughter ride in carts. Mind that 'ere lamp!'

Certainly a lamp had a very narrow escape, as trunk number one was brought to the ground with a crash, the second one being treated almost as mercilessly, but without a word from their owner, who quietly raising her veil and displaying a sweet sad face, now went to the pigeon-hole, regardless of the leering stare bestowed upon her by the exquisite, who had sauntered back into the booking-office.

' Third-class—London,' said the station-master aloud, repeating the fair young traveller's words. ' Nine-and-nine ;' and he too bestowed a not very respectful stare.

The threepence change was handed to the porter, with a request that he would see the boxes into the van, which request, and the money, that incorruptible gentleman received with a short nod and an ' all right,' pocketing the cash in defiance of all by-laws and ordinances of the company.

Turning to reach the platform, the young lady—for such her manners indicated her to be—became aware of the fixed insolent stare of the overdressed gentleman at her side, when quietly and without ostentation the black fall was lowered, and she walked slowly to and fro for a few minutes, in expectation of the coming train —hardly noticing that she was met at every turn, and that the gentlemanly manœuvres were being watched with great interest by station-master and porter.

' Nice day, deah!' was suddenly drawled out; and the traveller started to find that, in place of being met at every turn, her persecutor was now close by her side. Quickening her steps, she slightly bent her head and walked on; but in vain.

' Any one going to meet you ?' was next drawled out; when turning shortly round, the young traveller looked the ex-quisite full in the face.

' I think you are making a mistake, sir,' she said coldly.

' Mistake ? No, not I, my deah,'. was the insolent reply. ' Give me your ticket, and I'll change it;' and the speaker coolly held out a tightly-gloved hand.

The black veil hid the flush that rose to the pale face, as, glancing rapidly down the line for the train that seemed as if it

would never come, the traveller once more
quickened her steps and walked to the
other end of the platform; for there was
no waiting-room at the little wooden station, one but newly erected by way of ex-
periment.

' Now, don't be awkward, my deah,'
drawled the exquisite, once more overtak-
ing her. ' Here we are both going to town
together, and I can take care of you. Pretty
gyurls like you have no business to travel
alone. Now, let me change your ticket;'
and again he stretched forth his hand. ' I'll
pay, you know.'

' Are you a gentleman, sir?' was the
sudden question in reply to his proposition.

' Bai Jove, ya-a-a-s!' was the drawled
reply, accompanied by what was meant for
a most killing leer.

' Then you will immediately cease this
unmanly pursuit!' exclaimed the lady firm-

ly; and once more turning, she paced along
the platform.

'Now, how can you now,' languidly
whispered the self-styled gentleman, ' when
we might be so comfortable and chatty all
this long ride ? Look here, my deah—
take my arm, and I'll see to your luggage.'

As he spoke, with the greatest effrontery
he caught the young traveller's hand in
his, and drew it through his arm—the station-master and porter noting the perform-
ance, and nodding at one another; but the
next moment the former official changed
his aspect, for the hand was snatched away,
and the young lady hurried in an agitated
manner to the booking-office.

'Have you a room in which I could sit
down until the train comes?' she exclaimed.
'I am sorry to trouble you; but I am
travelling alone, and—'

'To be sure you are, my deah,' drawled

the persecutor, who had laughingly followed, ' when you have no business to do such a thing, and I won't allow it. It's all right, station - master — the train will be here directly. I'll see to the lady: friend of mine, in fact.'

' Indeed! I assure you, sir,' exclaimed the agitated girl, ' I do not know this gentleman. I appeal to you for protection.'

Here, in spite of her self-control, a sob burst from her breast.

' Here, this sort of thing won't do, sir,' said the youth, shaking his head. ' I can't allow it at my station. You mustn't annoy the lady, sir.' And turning very pink in the face, he tried to look important; but without success.

' I think you have the care of this station, have you not, my good lad?' drawled the exquisite.

' Yes, I have, sir,' was the reply, and

this time rather in anger, for the young
station-master hardly approved of being
called a 'good lad.'

'Then mind your station, boy, and don't
interfere.'

' Boy yourself, you confounded puppy!'
exclaimed the young fellow, firing up. 'I
never took any notice till the lady appealed
to me; but if she was my sister, sir, I'd—
I'd—I don't know what I wouldn't do to
you!'

' But you see she is not your sister; and
you are making a fool of yourself,' drawled
the other contemptuously.

.' Am I?' exclaimed the young man,
whose better nature was aroused. 'I consider that every lady who is being insulted
is the sister of an Englishman, and has a
right to his help. And now be off out of
this office, for I'm master here; and you
may report me if you like, for I don't

care who you are, nor yet if I lose my place.'

Red in the face, and strutting like a turkey-cock, the young man made at the dandy so fiercely, that he backed out on to the platform, to have the door banged after him so energetically, that one of the panes of glass was shivered to atoms.

' Come in here, miss, and I'll see that he don't annoy you again. Why didn't you speak sooner? Only wish I was going up to London, I'd see you safe home, that I would, miss; only, you see, I should lose my berth if I was absent without leave; and that wouldn't do, would it? May p'r'aps now, for that chap's a regular swell: come down here last week, and been staying at old Sir Henry Warr's, at the Beeches; but I don't care; I only did what was right —did I, miss?'

' Indeed, I thank you very, very much!'

exclaimed the protected one, holding out a little hand, which was eagerly seized. 'It was very kind; and I do sincerely hope I may not have been the cause—'

Here a sob choked further utterance.

'Don't you mind about that,' said the young man loftily, and feeling very exultant and self-satisfied. 'I'd lose half a dozen berths to please you, miss—I would, 'pon my word. Don't you take on about that. I'm your humble servant to command; and let's see if he'll speak to you again on my platform, that's all!'

Here the young man—very young man —breathed hard, stared hard, and blushed; for his anger having somewhat evaporated, he now began to think that he had been very chivalrous, and that he had fallen in love with this beautiful girl, whom it was his duty to protect evermore: feelings, however, not at all shared by the lady, who, though very grateful, was most earnestly wishing herself safely at her destination. The embarrassing position was, however, ended by the young station-master, who suddenly exclaimed:

'Here she comes!'

Then he led the way, pulling up his collar and scowling very fiercely till they reached the platform, where the exquisite was languidly pacing up and down.

'Now, you take my advice, miss,' said the protector: 'you jump into the first cab as soon as you get into the terminus, and have yourself driven home: I'll see that you ain't interfered with going up. I wish I was going with you; and, 'pon my word, miss, I should like to see you again.'

'Indeed, I thank you very much,' said the stranger. 'You have acted very nobly; and though you may never again be thanked by me, you will have the reward of know-

ing that you have protected a *sister* in distress.'

She laid a stress upon the word ' sister,'
as if referring to the young fellow's manly
reply to the dandy. But now ' she'—that
is to say, the train—had glided up, when,
turning smartly—

' See those boxes in, Joe !' exclaimed the
station-master; and then catching the traveller's hand in his, he led her to the guard.
' Put this young lady in a compartment
where there's more ladies,' he said. ' She's
going to London, and I want you to see
that she's safely off in a cab when she gets
there. She's my sister.'

' All right, Mr. Simpkin—all right,' said
the guard.

' Good-bye, miss—good-bye !' exclaimed
the young man confusedly, shaking her
hand. ' Business, you know—I must go.'

Just at that moment a thought seemed

to have struck the dandy, who made as if
to get to where the porter was thrusting
the two canvas - covered trunks into the
guard's van; but he was too late.

'Now, then, sir, if you're going on!'
exclaimed the station - master. 'Third-
class?' he asked by way of a sneer.

'Confound you! I'll serve you out for
this—bai Jove I will!' muttered the over-
dressed one, jumping hastily into a first-
class *coupé*, when, looking out, he had the
satisfaction of seeing the young station-
master spring on to the step of a third-class
carriage, and ride far beyond the end of
the platform, before he jumped down and
waved him a triumphant salute as the train
swept by.

The dandy made a point of going up to
that carriage at every stopping - station
where sufficient time was afforded; but the
fair young traveller sat with her face stu-

diously turned towards the opposite window.

'I've a good mind to ride third-class for
once in a way,' the gentleman muttered, as
he passed the carriage during one stoppage.

Just then a child cried out loudly; and
a soldier, smoking a dirty black pipe, thrust
his head out of the next compartment with
a 'How are you, matey?'

'Bai Jove, no! Couldn't do it!' murmured the exquisite, with a shudder; and
he returned to his seat, to look angry and
scowling for the rest of the journey.

He had made up his mind, though, as
to his proceedings when they reached London; but again he was doomed to disappointment; for on his approaching the object
of his pursuit in the crowd, he found the
stout guard a guard indeed in his care of
his charge; when, angrily turning upon his
heel, he made his way to the luggage-bar,

where, singling out the particular trunks
that he had seen at Littleborough, he
pressed through the throng, and eagerly
read one of the direction-labels.

' Bai Jove!' he exclaimed, with an air
of the most utter astonishment overspread-
ing his face ; and then again he read the
direction, but only again to give utterance
to his former ejaculation—' Bai Jove!'

He seemed so utterly taken aback that
he did not even turn angrily upon a porter
who jostled him, or upon another who with
one of the very boxes knocked his hat over
his eyes. The cab was laden and driven
off before his face so slowly that, once more
alone, he could have easily spoken to the
veiled occupant. But, no: he was so utterly astounded that when he hailed a han-
som, and slowly stepped in, his reply to
the driver as he peered down through the
little trap was only—

' Bai Jove!'

' Where to, sir?' said the man, astonished in his turn.

' Anywhere, my good fellow.'

' All right, sir.'

' No, no—stop. Drive me to the Wyndgate Club, St. James's-square.'

' All right, sir.'

And the cab drove off, with its occupant wondering and startled at the strange fashion in which every-day affairs will sometimes shape themselves, proving again and again how much more wild the truth can be than fiction, and musing upon what kind of an encounter his would be with the fair traveller when next he went home.

There was no record kept of the number of times the over-dressed gentleman gave utterance to that peculiarly-drawling exclamation; but it is certain that he startled his valet by jumping up suddenly at early morn from a dream of his encounter, to cry, as if disturbed by something almost painful:

'Who could have thought it? Bai Jove!'

CHAPTER III.

BLANDFIELD COURT.

'DID you ring, sir?' said a footman.

'Yes, Thomas. Go to Mr. Charles's room, and tell him that I should be glad of half an hour's conversation with him before he goes out, if he can make it convenient.'

The library-door of Blandfield Court closed; and after taking a turn or two up and down the room, Sir Philip Vining—a fine, florid, gray-headed old gentleman—stood for a moment gazing from the window at the sweep of park extending down to a glittering stream, which wound its way amidst glorious glades of beech and chestnut, bright in the virgin green of spring. But anxious of mien, and ill at ease, the old gentleman stepped slowly to the handsome carved-oak chair in which he had been seated, and then, intently watching the door, he leaned back, playing with his double gold eyeglass.

Five minutes passed, and then a step was heard crossing the hall—a step which made Sir Philip's face lighten up, as, leaning forward, a pleasant smile appeared upon his lip. Then a heavy bold hand was laid upon the handle, and the patient of Dr. Tiddson—fair, flushed, and open-countenanced—strode into the room, seeming as if he had brought with him the outer sunshine lingering in his bright brown hair and golden beard. He swung the door to with almost a bang; and then—free of gait, happy, and careless-looking, suffering from no broken rib, fractured clavicle, or concussed brain, as predicted three months before—he strode towards Sir Philip, who rose hurriedly with outstretched hands.

'My dear Charley, how are you this morning? You look flushed. Effects remaining of that unlucky fall, I'm afraid.'

'Fall? Nonsense, dad! Never better in my life,' laughed the young man, taking the outstretched hands and then subsiding into a chair. 'Mere trifle, in spite of the doctor's long phiz.'

'It is going back to old matters, but I'm very glad, my dear boy, that I saw Max Bray, and learned of your condition; and I've never said a word before, Charley, but why should you send for him in preference to your father?'

'Pooh!—nonsense, dad! First man I thought of. Did it to save you pain. Ought to have got up, and walked home. But there, let it pass. Mind my cigar?'

'No, no, my dear boy, of course

not,' said the old gentleman, coughing slightly. 'If it troubles me, I'll open the window.'

'But really, father,' said the young man, laying his hand tenderly on Sir Philip's arm, 'don't let me annoy you with my bad habit.'

'My dear boy, I don't mind. You know we old fogies used to have our bad habits—two bottles of port after dinner, to run down into our legs and make gouty pains, eh, Charley—eh? And look here, my dear boy—look here!'

Charley Vining laughed, and, leaning back in his chair, began to send huge clouds of perfumed smoke from his cabana, as his father drew out a handsome gold box, and took snuff à la courtier of George the Fourth's day.

'I don't like smoking, my boy; but it's better than our old drinking habits.'

' Hear—hear ! Cheers from the opposition !' laughed the son.

' Ah, my dear boy, why don't you give your mind to that sort of thing? Such a fine opening as there is in the county! Writtlum says they could get you in with a tremendous majority.'

' Parliament, dad? Nonsense! Pretty muff I should be ; get up to speak without half-a-dozen words to say.'

' Nonsense, Charley—nonsense ! The Vinings never yet disgraced their name.'

' Unworthy scion of the house, my dear father.'

' Now, my dear Charley !' exclaimed Sir Philip, as he looked with pride at the stalwart young fellow who was heir to his baronetcy and broad acres. ' But, let me see, my dear boy; John Martingale called yesterday while you were out. He says he has as fine a hunter as ever crossed coun-

try: good fencer, well up to your weight—
such a one as you would be proud of. I
told him to bring the horse on for you to
see; for I should not like you to miss a
really good hunter, Charley, and I might
be able to screw out a cheque.'

'My dear father,' exclaimed the young
man, throwing his cigar-end beneath the
grate, 'there really is no need. Martingale's a humbug, and only wants to palm
upon us some old screw. The mare is in
splendid order—quite got over my reckless
riding and the fall. I like her better every
day, and she'll carry me as much as I shall
want to hunt.'

'I'm glad you like her, Charley. You
don't think her to blame?'

'Blame? No! I threw her down. I
like her better every day, I tell you. But
you gave a cool hundred too much for her.'

'Never mind that. By the way, Char-

ley, Leathrum says they are hatching plenty
of pheasants: the spinneys will be full this
season; and I want you to have some good
shooting. The last poacher, too, has gone
from the village.'

'Who's that?' said Charley carelessly.

'Diggles—John Diggles. They brought
him before me for stealing pheasants' eggs,
and I—and I—'

'Well, what did you do, dad? Fine
him forty shillings?'

'Well, no, my boy. You see, he threw
himself on my mercy—said he'd such a
character no one would employ him, and
that he wanted to get out of the country; and that if he stopped he should
always be meddling with the game. And
you see, my dear boy, it's true enough;
so I promised to pay his passage to Ame-
rica.'

'A pretty sort of a county magistrate!'

laughed Charley. 'What do you think the reverend rectors, Lingon and Braceby, will say to you? Why, they would have given John Diggles a month.'

'Perhaps so, my dear boy; but the man has had no chance, and— No; sit still, Charley. I haven't done yet; I want to talk to you.'

'All right, dad. I was only going to give the mare a spin. Let her wait.' And he threw himself back in his chair.

'Yes, yes—let her wait this morning, my dear boy. But don't say " All right!" I don't like you to grow slangy, either in your speech or dress.' He glanced at the young man's easy tweed suit. 'That was one thing in which the old school excelled, in spite of their wine-bibbing propensities— they were particular in their language, dressed well, and were courtly to the other sex.'

' Yes,' yawned Charley; 'but they were dreadful prigs.'

' Perhaps so—perhaps so, my dear boy,' said the old gentleman, laying his hand upon his son's knee. 'But do you know, Charley, I should like to see you a little more courtly and attentive to—to the la-dies ?'

' I adore that mare you gave me, dad.'

' Don't be absurd. I want to see you more in ladies' society; so polishing—so improving!'

' Hate it!' said Charley laconically.

' Nonsense—nonsense! Now look here!'

' No, dad. Look here,' said Charley, leaning towards his father and gazing full in his face with a half-serious, half-banter-ing smile lighting up his clear blue eye. ' You're beating about the bush, dad, and the bird won't start. You did not send for me to say that Martingale had been about a horse, or Leathrum had hatched so many pheasants, or that Diggles was going to leave the country. Frankly, now, governor, what's in the wind ?'

Sir Philip Vining looked puzzled; he threw himself back in his chair, took snuff hastily, spilling a few grains upon his cambric shirt-frill. Then, with his gold-box in his left hand, he bent forward and laid his right upon the young man's ample breast, gazing lovingly in his face, and said:

'Frankly, then, my dear Charley, I want to see you married!'

CHAPTER IV.

CONCERNING MATRIMONY.

CHARLES VINING gazed half laughingly in his father's earnest face ; then throwing himself back, he burst into an uncontrolled fit of merriment.

'Ha, ha, ha! Me married! Why, my dear father, what next?' Then, seeing the look of pain in Sir Philip's countenance, he rose and stood by his side, resting one hand upon his shoulder. 'Why, my dear father,' he said, 'what ever put that in your head? I never even thought of such a thing!'

'My dear boy, I know it—I know it; and that's why I speak. You see, you are now just twenty-seven, and a fine hand-some young fellow—'

Charley made a grimace.

'While I am getting an old man, Charley, and the time cannot be so very far off before I must go to my sleep. You are my only child, and I want the Squire of Blandfield to keep up the dignity of the old family. Don't interrupt me, my boy, I have not done yet. I must soon go the way of all flesh—'

'Heaven forbid!' said Charley fervently.

'And it is the dearest wish of my heart to see you married to some lady of good birth—one who shall well do the honours of your table. Blandfield must not pass to a collateral branch, Charley; we must have an heir to these broad acres; for I hope the time will come, my boy, when in this very library you will be seated, gray and aged as I am, talking to some fine stalwart son, who, like you, shall possess his

dear mother's eyes, ever to bring to remembrance happy days gone by, my boy—
gone by never to return.'

The old man's voice trembled as he
spoke, and the next moment his son's
hands were clasped in his, while as eye
met eye there was a weak tear glistening
in that of the elder, and the lines seemed
more deeply cut in his son's fine open
countenance.

'My dear father!' said the young man
softly.

'My dear Charley!' said Sir Philip.

There was silence for a while as father
and son thought of the days of sorrow ten
years back, when Blandfield Court was
darkened, and steps passed lightly about
the fine old mansion, because its lady—
loved of all for miles round — had been
suddenly called away from the field of la-
bour that she had blessed. And then they

looked up to the portrait gazing down at them from the chimneypiece, seeming almost to smile sadly upon them as they watched the skilful limning of the beloved features.

A few moments after, a smile dawned upon the old man's quivering lip, as, still retaining his son's hand, he motioned him to take a seat by his side.

'My dear Charley,' he said at last, 'I think you understand my wishes.'

'My dear father, yes.'

'And you will try?'

'To gratify you?—Yes, yes, of course; but really, father—'

'My dear boy, I know—I know what you would say. But look here, Charley— there has always been complete confidence between us; is there—is there anything?'

'Any lady in the case? What, any tender *penchant?*' laughed Charley. 'My dear father, no. I think I've hardly given a thought to anything but my horses and dogs.'

'I'm glad of it, Charley, I'm glad of it! And now let's quietly chat it over. Do you know, my dear boy, that you are shutting yourself out from an Eden? Do you not believe in love?'

'Well, ye-e-es. I believe that you and my dear mother were most truly happy.'

'We were, my dear boy, we were. And why should not you be as happy?'

'Hem!' ejaculated Charley; and then firmly: 'Because, sir, I believe that there is not such a woman as my dear mother upon earth.'

The old gentleman shaded his eyes for a few moments with his disengaged hand.

'Frankly again, father,' said the young man, 'is there a lady in view?'

'Well, no, my dear boy, not exactly; but I certainly was talking with Bray over our port last week, when we perhaps did agree that you and Laura seemed cut out for one another; but, my dear boy, don't think I want to play the tyrant and choose for you. They do say, though, that the lady has a leaning your way; and no wonder, Charley, no wonder!'

'I don't know very much about Laura,' said Charley musingly. 'She's a fine girl certainly; looks rather Jewish, though, with those big red lips of hers and that hooked nose.'

'My dear Charley!' remonstrated Sir Philip.

'But she rides well—sits that great rawboned mare of hers gloriously. I saw her take a leap on the last day I was out —one that I took too, about half an hour before that fall; but hang me if it wasn't to avoid being outdone by a woman! I really wanted to shirk it.'

'Good, good!' laughed Sir Philip.

'But she's fast, and not feminine, to my way of thinking,' said Charley, gazing up as he spoke at the picture above the mantelpiece, and comparing the lady in question with the truly gentle mother whom he had almost worshipped. 'She burst out with a hoarse "Bravo!" when she saw me safely landed, and then shouted, "Well done, Charley!" and I felt so nettled, that I pulled out my cigar-case, and asked her to take one.'

'But she did not?' exclaimed Sir Philip.

'Well, no,' said Charley, 'she did not, certainly—she only laughed; but she looked just as if she were half disposed. She's one of your Spanish style of women: scents, too, tremendously—bathes in Ihlang-Ihlang, I should think; perhaps because she delights in garlic and onions, and wants to smother the odour!'

'My dear boy—my dear boy!' laughed Sir Philip, 'you do really want polish horribly! What a way to speak of a lady! It's terrible, you know! But there, don't judge harshly, and you are perfectly unfettered; only just bear this in mind: it would give me great pleasure if you were to lead Laura Bray in here some day and say— But there, you know—you know! Still I place no tie upon you, Charley: only bring me some fair sweet girl—by birth a lady, of whom I can be proud—and then all I want is that you shall give me a chair at your table and fireside. You might have the title if it were possible, but you shall have the Court and the income—everything. Only let me have my glass of wine and my bit of snuff, and play with your children. Heaven bless you, my dear boy!

I'll go off the bench directly, and you shall be a county magistrate; but you must be married, Charley—you must be married!'

Charley Vining did not appear to be wonderfully elated by his future prospects, for, sighing, he said:

'Really, father, I could have been very happy to have gone on just as we are; but your wishes—'

'Yes, my dear boy, my wishes. And you will try? Only don't bother yourself; take time, and mix a little more with society—accept a few more invitations—go to a few of the archery and croquet parties.'

'Heigho, dad!' sighed Charley. 'Why, I should be sending arrows for fun in the stout old dowagers' backs, and breaking the slow curates' shins with my croquet mallet! There, leave me to my own devices, and I'll see what I can do!'

'To be sure—to be sure, Charley! And you do know Maximilian Bray?'

'Horrid snob!' laughed Charley, 'such a languid swell! Do you know what our set call him? But there, of course you don't! "Donkey Bray" or else "Long-ears!"'

'There, there—never mind that! I don't want you to marry him, Charley. And there—there's Beauty at the door!' exclaimed the old gentleman, shaking his son's hand. 'Go and have your ride, Charley! Good-bye! But you'll think of what I said?'

'I will, honestly,' said the young man.

'And—stay a moment, Charley: Lex-ville flower-show is to-morrow. I can't go. Couldn't you, just to oblige me? I like to see these affairs patronised; and Pruner takes a good many of our things over. He generally carries off a few prizes. I see

they've quite stripped the conservatory.
You'll go for me, won't you?'

'Yes, father, if you wish it,' sighed
Charley.

'I do wish it, my dear boy; but don't
sigh, pray!'

'All right, dad,' said the young man,
brightening, and shaking Sir Philip's hand,
'I'll go; give away the prizes, too, if they
ask me,' he laughed. And the next moment the door closed upon his retreating
form.

Sir Philip Vining listened to his son's
departing step, and then muttering, 'They
will ask him too,' he rose, and went to the
window, from which he could just get a
glimpse of the young man mounting at the
hall-door. The next moment Charley cantered by upon a splendid roan mare, turning her on to the lawn-like sward, and dis-
appearing behind a clump of beeches.

'He's a noble boy!' muttered the father proudly; and then as he walked thoughtfully back to his chair, 'A fine dashing fellow!'

But of course these were merely the fond expressions of a weak parent.

CHAPTER V.

CHARLEY'S ENCOUNTERS.

'Bai Jove, Vining! that you?' languidly exclaimed a little, thin, carefully-dressed man, ambling gently along on one of the most thoroughly-broken of ladies' mares, whose pace was so easy that not a curl of her master's jetty locks was disarranged, or a crease formed in his tightly-buttoned surtout. His figure said 'stays' as plainly as figure could speak; he wore an eyeglass screwed into the brim of his very glossy hat; his eyes were half closed; his moustache was waxed and curled up at the ends like old-fashioned skates; and his carefully-trained whiskers lightly brushed their tips against his shoulders. And to set off such arrangements to the greatest advantage, he displayed a great deal of white wristband and shirt-front; his collar came down into the sharpest of peaks; and he rode in lemon-kid gloves and patent-leather boots.

' Hallo, Max!' exclaimed Charley, looking like some Colossus as he reined in by the side of the dandy, who was going in the same direction along a shady lane. ' How are you? When did you come down?'

' So, so—so, so, mai dear fellow! Came down la-a-ast night. But pray hold in that confounded great beast of yours: she's making the very deuce of a dust! I shall be covered!'

Charley patted and soothed his fiery curveting steed into a walk, which was quite sufficient to keep it abreast of Maximilian Bray's ambling jennet, which kept up a dancing, circus - horse motion, one evidently approved by its owner for its aid in displaying his graceful horsemanship.

'Nice day,' said Charley, scanning with a side glance his companion's 'get-up,' and evidently with a laughing contempt.

'Ya-a-s, nice day,' drawled Bray, 'but confoundedly dusty!'

'Rain soon,' said Charley maliciously. 'Lay it well.'

'Bai Jove, no—surely not!' exclaimed the other, displaying a great deal of trepidation. 'You don't think so, do you?'

'Black cloud coming up behind,' said Charley coolly.

'Bai Jove, mai dear fellow, let's push on and get home! You'll come and lunch, won't you?'

'No, not to-day,' said Charley. 'But I'm going into the town to see the saddler. I'll ride with you.'

'Tha-a-anks!' drawled Bray, with a grin

of misery. 'But, mai dear fellow, hadn't
you better go on the grass? You're covering me with dust!'

'Confounded puppy! Nice brother-in-
law! Wring his neck!' muttered Charley,
as he turned his mare on to the grass which
skirted the side of the road, as did Bray on
the other, when, the horses' paces being
muffled by the soft turf, conversation was
renewed.

'Bai Jove, Vining, you'll come over to
the flower-show to-morrow, won't you?
There'll be some splendid girls there! Good
show too, for the country. You send a lot
of things, don't you?—Covent-garden stuff
and cabbages, eh?'

'Humph!' growled Charley 'The governor's going to have some sent, I s'pose;
our gardener's fond of that sort of thing.
Think perhaps I shall go.'

'Ya-a-s, I should go if I were you. It

does you country fellows a deal of good, I always think, to get into society.'

'Does it?' said Charley, raising his eye-brows a little.

'Bai Jove, ya-a-s! You'd better go. Laura's going, and the Lingon's girls are coming to lunch. You'd better come over to lunch and go with us,' drawled the exquisite.

'Well, I don't know,' said Charley, hesitating; for he was thinking whether it would not be better than going quite alone—' I don't know what to say.'

'Sa-a-ay? Sa-a-ay ya-a-s,' drawled Bray. 'Come in good time and have a weed first in my room; and then we'll taste some sherry the governor has got da-awn. He always leaves it till I come da-awn from ta-awn. Orders execrable stuff himself, as I often tell him. Wouldn't have a drop fit to drink if it weren't for me. You'd better come.'

'Well, really,' said Charley again, half mockingly, 'I don't know what to say.'

'Why, sa-a-ay ya-a-as, and come.'

'Well, then, "ya-a-as"!' drawled Charley, in imitation of the other's tone.

But Maximilian Bray's skin was too thick for the little barb to penetrate; and he rode gingerly on, petting his whiskers, and altering the sit of his hat; when, being thoroughly occupied with his costume, horse and man nearly came headlong to the ground, in consequence of the mare stumbling over a small heap of road-scrapings. But the little animal saved herself, though only by a violent effort, which completely unseated Maximilian Bray, who was thrown forward upon her neck, his hat being dislodged and falling with a sharp bang into the dusty road.

'All right! No bones broken! You've better luck than I have!' laughed Charley, as he fished up the fallen hat with his hunting-whip. 'Nip her well with your knees, man, and then you won't be unseated again in that fashion. Here, take your hat.'

'Bai Jove!' ejaculated the breathless dandy, 'it's too bad! That fellow who left the sweepings by the roadside ought to be shot! Mai dear fellow, your governor, as a magistrate, ought to see to it! Tha-a-anks!'

He took his hat, and began ruefully to wipe off the dust with a scented handkerchief before again covering his head; but though he endeavoured to preserve an outward appearance of calm, there was wrath in his breast as he gazed down at one lemon-coloured tight glove split to ribbons, and a button burst away from his surtout coat. He could feel too that his moustache was coming out of curl, and it only wanted the sharp shower which now came pattering down to destroy the last remains of his equanimity.

'Bai Jove, how beastly unfortunate!' he exclaimed, urging his steed into a smart canter.

'Well, I don't know,' said Charley coolly, in his rough tweed suit that no amount of rain would have injured. 'Better to-day than to-morrow. Do no end of good, and bring on the hay.'

'Ya-a-as, I suppose so,' drawled Bray; 'but do a confounded deal of harm!' and he gazed at the sleeves of his glossy Saville-row surtout.

'O, never mind your coat, man!' laughed Charley. 'See how it lays the dust!'

'Ya-a-as, just so,' drawled Bray. 'I shall take this short cut and get home. Only a shower! Bye-bye! See you to-morrow! Come to lunch.'

The ragged lemon glove was waved to

Charley as its owner turned down a side lane; and now that his costume was completely disordered and wet, he made no scruple about digging his spurs into his mare's flanks, and galloping homewards; while, heedless of the sharply-falling rain, Charley gently cantered on towards the town.

' Damsels in distress!' exclaimed the young man suddenly. ' " Bai Jove!" as Longears says. Taken refuge from the rain beneath a tree! Leaves, young and weak, completely saturated — impromptu shower - bath! What shall I do? Lend them my horse? No good. They would not ride double, like Knight Templars. Ride off, then, for umbrellas, I suppose. Why didn't that donkey stop a little longer? and then he could have done it.'

So mused Charley Vining as he cantered up to where, beneath a spreading elm by

the road-side, two ladies were waiting the
cessation of the rain—faring, though, very
little better than if they had stood in the
open. One was a fashionably-dressed, tall,
dark, bold beauty, black of eye and tress,
and evidently in anything but the best of
tempers with the weather; the other a fair
pale girl, in half-mourning, whose yellow
hair was plainly braided across her white
forehead, but only to be knotted together
at the back in a massive cluster of plaits,
which told of what a glorious golden mantle
it could have shed over its owner, rippling
down far below the waist, and ready, it
seemed, to burst from prisoning comb and
pin. There was something ineffably sweet
in her countenance, albeit there was a subdued, even sorrowful look as her shapely
little head was bent towards her companion,
and she was evidently speaking as Charley
cantered up.

'Sorry to see you out in this, Miss Bray,' he cried, raising his low-crowned hat. 'What can I do?—Fetch umbrellas and shawls? Speak the word.'

'O, how kind of you, Mr. Vining!' exclaimed the dark maiden, with brightening eyes and flushing cheeks. 'But really I should not like to trouble you.'

'Trouble? Nonsense!' cried Charley. 'Only speak before you get wet through.'

'Well, if you really—really, you know —would not mind,' hesitated Laura Bray, who, in spite of the rain, was in no hurry to bring the interview to a close.

'Wouldn't mind? Of course not!' echoed Charley, whose bold eyes were fixed upon Laura Bray's companion, who timidly returned his salute, and then shrank back, as he again raised his little deer-stalker hat from its curly throne. 'Now, then,' he exclaimed, 'what's it to be?—shawls and Sairey Gamps of gingham and tape?'

'No, no, Mr. Vining! How droll you are!' laughed the beauty. 'But if you really wouldn't mind—really, you know—'

'I, tell, you, Miss, Bray, that, I, shall, only, be, too, happy,' said Charley, in measured tones.

'Then, if you wouldn't mind riding to the Elms, and asking them to send the brougham, I should be so much obliged!'

'All right!' cried Charley, turning his mare. 'Max has only just left me.'

'But it seems such a shame to send you away through all this rain!' said Laura loudly.

'Fudge!' laughed Charley, as, putting his mare at the hedge in front, she skimmed over it like a bird, and her owner galloped across country, to the great disadvantage of several crops of clover.

'What a pity!' sighed Laura to herself, as she watched the retreating form. 'And the rain will be over directly. I wonder whether he'll come back!'

'Do you think we need wait?' said her companion gently. 'The rain has ceased now, and the sun is breaking through the clouds.'

'O, of course, Miss Bedford!' said Laura pettishly. 'It would be so absurd if the carriage came and found us gone;' when, seeing that the dark beauty evidently wished to be alone with her thoughts, the other remained silent.

'Who in the world can that be with her?' mused Charley, as he rode along. 'Might have had the decency to introduce me, anyhow. Don't know when I've seen a softer or more gentle face. Splendid hair too! No sham there : no fear of her moulting a curl here and a tress there, if her back hair came undone. No, she don't seem as if there were any sham about her—quiet, ladylike, and nice. 'Pon my word, I believe Laura Bray would make a better man than Max. Seem to like those silver-gray dresses with a black-velvet jacket, they look so—There, what a muff 1 am, going right out of the way, while that little darling is getting wet as a sponge! Easy, lass! Now, then—over!' he cried to his mare, as she skimmed another hedge. ' Wonder what her name is! Some visitor come to the flower-show, I suppose—*fiancée* of Longears probably. Steady, then, Beauty!' he cried again to the mare, who, warming to her work, was beginning to tear furiously over the ground ; for, pre-occupied by thought, Charley had inadvertently been using his spurs pretty freely.

But he soon reduced his steed to a state of obedience, and rode on, musing upon his late encounter.

'Can't be!' he thought. 'A girl with a head like that would never take up with such a donkey! Ah, there he goes, drenched like a rat! Ha, ha, ha! How miserably disgusted the puppy did look! Patronising me, too—a gnat! Advising me to go into society, et cætera! Well, I can't help it: I do think him a conceited ass! But perhaps, after all, he thinks the same of me; and I deserve it.

'Dear old dad,' he mused again after awhile. 'Like to see me married and settled, would he? What should I be married for?—a regular woman-hater! Why, in the name of all that's civil, didn't Laura introduce me to that little blonde? Like to know who she is—not that it matters to me! Over again, my lass!' he cried, patting the mare as she once more bounded over a hedge, this time to drop into a lane straight as a line, and a quarter of a mile

down which Maximilian Bray could be seen
hurrying along—Charley's short cut across
the fields having enabled him to gain upon
the fleeing dandy.

'May as well catch up to him, and tell
him what I've seen,' said Charley, urging
on his mare. ' No, I won't,' he said, checking. ' Better too, perhaps. No, I won't.
Why should I send the donkey back to
them ? Not much fear, though : he'll be
too busy for a couple of hours restoring
his damaged plumes—a conceited popin-
jay!'

He cantered gently on now, seeming to
take the shower with him, for he could see,
on turning, that it was getting fine and
bright. But the rain had quite ceased as
he rode up to the door of the Brays' seat—
a fine old red-brick mansion known as the
Elms—just as a groom was leading the
ambling palfrey to its stable at the King's

Arms — there not being accommodation
in the paternal stables—a steed not much
more than half the size of the great rawboned
hunter favoured by Max's masculine sister.

'Why, here's Mr. Charley Vining!' cried
a shrill loud voice, from an open window.
'How de do, Mr. Vining—how de do?
Come to lunch, haven't you? So glad!
And so sorry Laura isn't at home! Caught
in the shower, I'm afraid.'

The owner of the voice appeared at the
window, in the shape of a very big bony
lady in black satin—bony not so much in
figure as in face, which seemed fitted with
too much skull, displaying a great deal of
cheek prominence, and a macaw-beaked
nose, with the skin stretched over it very
tightly, forming on the whole an organ of
a most resonant character—one that it was
necessary to hear before it could be thoroughly believed in. In fact, with all due

reverence to a lady's nose, it must be stated that the one in question acted as a sort of war-trump, which Mrs. Bray blew with masculine force when about to engage in battle with husband or servant for some case of disputed supremacy.

'Ring the bell, girls,' shrieked the lady; 'and let some one take Mr. Vining's horse. Do come in, Mr. Vining!'

'How do, Vining—how do?' cried a little pudgy man, appearing at the window, but hardly visible beside his lady—Mrs. Bray in more ways than one eclipsing her lord. 'How do? How's Sir Philip?'

'Quite well, thanks; but not coming in,' cried Charley, from his horse's back. 'Miss Bray and some lady caught in the rain—under tree—bad shelter—want the brougham.'

'Dear me, how tiresome!' screamed Mrs. Bray. 'But must we send it, Ness?'

Mr. Bray, named at his baptism Onesimus, replied by stroking his cheek and looking thoughtfully at his lady.

'The rain's about over now, and they might surely walk,' shrieked Mrs. Bray. 'Dudgeon grumbles so, too, when he has to go out like this, and he was ordered for two o'clock.'

'Better send, my dear,' whispered Mr. Bray, with a meaning look. 'Vining won't like it if you don't.'

Mrs. Bray evidently approved of her husband's counsel; for orders were given that the brougham should be in immediate readiness.

'They won't be long,' she now screamed, all smiles once more. 'But do come in and have some lunch, Mr. Vining : don't sit there in your wet clothes.'

'No—no. I'm all right,' cried Charley. 'I'm off again directly.'

But for all that, he lingered.

'You'll be at the flower-show to-morrow, won't you?' said Mrs. Bray.

'Well, yes, I think I shall go,' said Charley. 'I suppose everybody will be there.'

'O, of course; Laura's going. I suppose you send some things from the Court?'

'Yes,' said Charley; but he added, laughing, 'What will be the use, when you are going to send such a prize blossom?'

'For shame, you naughty man!' said Mrs. Bray. 'I shall certainly tell Laura you've turned flatterer.'

'I say, Charley Vining,' squeaked a loud voice from the next window, 'we're going to beat you Court folks.'

'We are, are we?' laughed Charley, turning in the direction of the voice, which proceeded from a very tall angular young lady of sixteen—a tender young plant, nearly all stem, and displaying very little blossom or leaf. She was supported on either side by two other tender plants, of fourteen and twelve respectively, forming a trio known at the Elms as 'the children.' 'I'm very glad to hear it, Miss Nell; but suppose we wait till after the judge's decision. But there goes the carriage. Goodbye, all!'

And turning his horse's head, he soon overtook the brougham, when, after soothing Mr. Dudgeon, the driver, with a shilling, the progress was pretty swift until they reached the tree, where, now finding shelter from the sun instead of the rain, yet stood Laura Bray and her companion.

'O, how good of you, Mr. Vining! and to come back, too!' gushed Laura, with sparkling eyes. 'I shall never be out of debt, I'm sure. I don't know what I should have done if it had not been for you!'

'Walked home, and a blessed good job, too!' muttered Mr. John Dudgeon.

'Don't name it!' said Charley. 'Almost a pity it's left off raining.'

'For shame—no! How can you talk so!' exclaimed Laura, shaking her sunshade at the speaker. 'But I really am so much obliged—I am indeed!'

Charley dismounted and opened the carriage-door, handing in first Miss Bray, who stepped forward, leaned heavily upon his arm, and then took her place, arranging her skirts so as to fill the back seat, talking gushingly the while as she made play at Charley with her great dark eyes.

But the glances were thrown away, Charley's attention being turned to her companion, who bent slightly, just touched the proffered hand, and stepped into the brougham, taking her seat with her back to the horse.

'So much obliged—so grateful!' cried Laura, as Charley closed the door. 'I shall never be able to repay you, I'm sure. Thanks! So much! Good-bye! See you at the flower-show to-morrow, of course? Good-bye!—*good*-bye!'

'She's getting a precious deal too affectionate! Talk about wanting me to marry *her*, why she'll run away with *me* directly!' grumbled Charley, as Mr. Dudgeon impatiently drove off, leaving the young man with the impression of a swiftly passing vision of Laura Bray showing her white teeth in a great smile as she waved her hand, and of a fair gentle face bent slightly down, so that he could see once more the rich massive braids resting upon a shapely, creamy neck. 'Have they been saying anything to her?' said Charley, as the brougham disappeared. 'She's getting quite unpleasant. Grows just like the old wo-

man: regularly parrot-beaked. Why didn't
she introduce me? Took the best seat, too!
Looks strange! I say, though, "bai Jove!"
—as that sweet brother says—this sort of
thing won't do! I should like to please
the dad; but I don't think I could manage
to do it "that how," as they say about here.
She quite frightens me! Heigho! what a
bother life is when you can't spend it just
as you like! Wish I was out in Australia
or Africa, or somewhere to be free and
easy—to hunt and shoot and ride as one
liked. Let's see: I shall not go over to
the town now—it's nearly lunch-time, and
I'm wet.'

He had mounted his horse, and was
about to turn homeward, when something
shining in the grass caught his eye, and
leaping down, he snatched up from among
the glistening strands, heavy with rain-
drops, a little golden cross—one that had

evidently slipped from velvet or ribbon as the ladies stood beneath that tree.

'That's not Miss Laura's—can't be!' muttered Charley, as he gazed intently at the little ornament. 'Not half fine enough for her.'

Then turning it over, he found engraved upon the reverse:

'*E. B. From her Mother*, 1860.'

'E. B.—E. B.—E. B.! And pray who is E. B.?' muttered Charley, as, once more mounting, he turned his horse's head homeward. 'Eleanor B. or Eliza—no, that's a housemaid's name—Ernestine, Eva. Who can she be? Not introduced—given the back seat—hardly spoken to, and yet so ladylike, and— There, get on, Beauty! What am I thinking about? We sha'n't be back to lunch.'

He cantered on for a mile; and then as

they entered a sunny lane—a very arcade
of gem-besprinkled verdure—he drew rein,
and taking the little cross from his pocket,
once more read the inscription.

' " E. B. From her mother, 1860."
And pray who is her mother? and who is
E. B.? Nobody from about here, I'll be
bound. But what a contrast to that great,
tall, dark woman! And they call her beautiful! Not half so beautiful as you, my
lass!' he cried, rousing himself, and patting
his mare's arched neck. 'You are my
beauty, eh, lass? Get on, then!'

But as Charley Vining rode on he grew
thoughtful, and more than once he absently
muttered:

'Yes; I think I'll go to the flower-show
to-morrow!'

CHAPTER VI.

A SECOND MEETING.

MAXIMILIAN BRAY, Esq., clerk in her Majesty's Treasury, Whitehall, sat in his dressing-room soured and angry. He had been hard at work trying to restore the mischief done by the rain; but in spite of 'Bandoline' and 'Brilliantine,' he could not get hair, moustache, or whiskers to take their customary curl: they would look limp and dejected. Then that superfine coat was completely saturated with water, as was also his hat, neither of which would, he knew, ever again display the pristine gloss. And, besides, he had been unseated before 'that coarse boor, Charley Vining,' and the fellow had had the impertinence to grin.

But, there, what could you expect from such a country clown? Altogether, Maximilian Bray, Esq., was cross—not to say savage— and more than once he had caught himself biting his nails—another cause for annoy- ance, since he was very careful with those almond-shaped nails, and had to pare, file, and burnish them afterwards to remove the inequality.

The above causes for a disordered tem- per have been recorded; but they were far from all. It is said that it never rains but it pours, and as that was the case out of doors, so it was in. But it would be wearisome to record the breaking of boot- loops, the tearing out of shirt-buttons, and the crowning horror of a spot of ironmould right in the front of the principal plait. Suffice it that Maximilian Bray felt as if he could have quarrelled with the whole world; and as he sat chilled with his wet-

ting, he had hard work to keep from gnawing his finger-nails again and again.

He might have gone down into the
drawing-room, warm with the sun, while
his northern-aspected window lent no genial
softness; but no: there was something on
his mind; and though he was dressed, he
lingered still.

He knew that the luncheon bell would
ring directly; in fact, he had referred several times to his watch. But still he hung
back, as if shrinking from some unpleasant
task, till, nerving himself, he rose and went
to the looking-glass, examining himself
from top to toe, grinning to see if his teeth
were perfectly white, dipping a corner of
the towel in water to remove the faintest
suspicion of a little cherry tooth-paste from
the corner of his mouth, biting his lips to
make them red, trying once more to give
his lank moustache the customary curl, but

trying in vain—in short, going through the varied acts of a man who gives the whole of his mind to his dress; and then, evidently thoroughly dissatisfied, he strode across the room, flung open the door, and began to descend the stairs.

The builder of the Elms, not being confined for space, had made on the first floor a long passage, upon which several of the bedrooms opened; and this passage, being made the receptacle for the cheap pictures purchased at sales by Mr. Onesimus Bray, was known in the house as the 'long gallery.'

Descending a short flight of stairs, Maximilian Bray was traversing this gallery, when the encounter which in his heart of hearts he had been dreading ever since he came down the night before was forced upon him; for, turning into the passage from the other end, the companion of

Laura Bray's morning walk came hurriedly along, slackening her pace, though, as she perceived that there was a stranger in advance; but as their eyes met, a sudden start of surprise robbed the poor girl for a few moments of her self-control; the blood flushed to her temples, and for an instant she stopped short.

But Maximilian Bray was equal to the occasion. He had fought off the encounter as long as he could; but now that the time had come, he had determined upon brazening it out.

'Ha, ha!' he laughed playfully. 'Know me again, then? Quite frightened you, didn't I? Shouldn't have been so cross last time, when I only wanted to see you safe on your journey. Didn't know who I was, eh? But, bai Jove! glad to see you again—am indeed!'

There was no reply for an instant to

these greetings. But as the flush faded, to
leave the face of her to whom they were
addressed pale and stern, Maximilian Bray's
smile grew more and more forced. The
words were too shallow of meaning not to
be rightly interpreted; and overcoming the
surprise that had for a few moments fet-
tered her, the fair girl turned upon Bray a
keen piercing look, as moving forward she
slightly bent, and said coldly in her old
words:

'I think, sir, you have made some mistake.'

'Mistake? No! Stop a minute. No
mistake, bai Jove—no! You remember me,
of course, when I startled you at the station. Only my fun, you know, only that
young donkey must interfere. Glad to see
you again — am, indeed, bai Jove! We
shall be capital friends, I know.'

As he spoke, he stepped before his com-

panion, arresting her progress, and holding
out his hand.

Driven thus to bay, the young girl
once more turned and faced her pursuer
with a look so firm and piercing, that
he grew discomposed, and the words
he uttered were unconnected and stam-
mering.

'Sorry, you know, bai Jove! Mistook
my meaning. Glad to see you again—am,
bai Jove! Eh? What say?'

'I was not aware that Mr. Maximilian Bray and the gentleman'—she laid
a hardly perceptible emphasis on the word
'gentleman'—'whom I encountered at that
country station were the same. Allow
me to remind you, sir, that you made
a mistake then in addressing a stranger.
You make another error in addressing
me again; for bear in mind we are stran-
gers yet. Excuse me for saying so, but

I think it would be better to forget the past.'

'Ya-as, just so—bai Jove! yes. It was nothing, you know, only—'

Maximilian Bray stopped short, for the simple reason that he was alone; for, turning hastily, his companion had retraced her steps, leaving the exquisite son of the house —the pride of his mother, the confidant of his sister, and the pest of the servants— looking quite 'like a fool, you know, bai Jove!'

They were his own words, though meant for no other ears but his own, being a little too truthful. Then he stood thinking and gnawing one nail for a few moments before continuing his way down to the dining-room.

'So we are to be as if we met for the first time, are we?' he muttered; and then his countenance lighted up into an inane smile as he thought to himself, 'Well, I've got it over. And, after all, it's something like being taken into her confidence, for haven't we between us what looks uncommonly like a secret?'

CHAPTER VII.

A DAWNING SENSE.

They were rather famous for their flower-shows at Lexville, not merely for the capital displays of Nature's choicest beauties, educated by cunning floriculturists to the nearest point to perfection, but also for their wet days. When the exhibition was first instituted, people said that the marquee was soaked and the ladies' dresses spoiled, simply because the show was held upon a Friday. 'Just,' they said, 'as if anybody but a committee would have chosen a Friday for an outdoor fête!'

But, if anything, the day was a little worse upon the next occasion, when Thursday had been selected, the same fate attending the luckless managers upon a Monday, a Tuesday, and a Wednesday. But now at last it seemed as if the fair goddess Flora herself had enlisted the sympathies of that individual known to mortals as 'the clerk of the weather,' and, in consequence, the day was all that could be desired. In fact, the weather was so fine, that the bandsmen of the Grenadier Guards, instead of coming down in their old and tarnished uniforms— declared, as a rule, to be good enough for Lexville—mustered in full force, gorgeous in their brightest scarlet and gold. The committee-men had shaken hands in the secretary's tent a dozen times over as many glasses of sherry, and forgotten to eat their biscuits in their hurry to order the cords of Edgington's great tent to be tightened, so potent were the rays of the sun; while within the canvas palace, in a golden hazy shade, the floral beauties from many a hot-house and conservatory were receiving the last touches by way of arrangement.

Lexville was in a profound state of excitement that day, and Miss l'Aiguille, the dressmaker, declared that she had been nearly torn to pieces by her customers.

'As for Miss Bray,' she said, 'not another dress would she make for her—no, not if she became bankrupt to-morrow—that she wouldn't! Six tryings-on, indeed, and then not satisfied!'

However, Miss l'Aiguille's troubles were so far over that, like the rest of Lexville, she had partaken of an early dinner, or lunch, and prepared herself to visit the great fête.

Lexville flower-show was always held in the grounds of one of the county magistrates, the Rev. Henry Lingon, concerning whose kindness the reporter for the little newspaper generally went into raptures in print, and received orders for half-a-dozen extra copies the next bench-day. And now fast and furiously the carriages began to set down—the wealth and fashion of the neighbourhood making a point of being the earlier arrivals, so as to miss the crowd of commoner beings who would afterwards flock together.

'Ah, Vining! You're here, then, mai dear fellow! Why didn't you come to lunch?' exclaimed Maximilian Bray, sauntering up to the young man, who, rather flushed and energetic, was talking to a knot of flower-button-holed committee-men.

'How do, Max?' exclaimed Charley, hastily taking the extended hand, and giving it a good shake. Then, turning to the committee-men: 'Much rather not—would, really, you know—don't feel myself adapted. Well, there,' he exclaimed at last, in answer to several eager protestations, 'I'll do it, if

you can get no one else!—Want me to
give away the prizes,' he said, turning to
Max Bray, who was gazing ruefully at his
right glove, in whose back a slight crack
was visible, caused, no doubt, by the hearty
but rough grasp it had just received.

'To be sure—of course!' drawled Bray.
'You're the very man, bai Jove! But
won't you come towards the gate? I expect our people here directly.'

Nothing loth, Vining strolled with his
companion down one of the pleasant floral
avenues, but seeing no flowers, hearing no
band; for his gaze, he hardly knew why,
was directed towards the approach; and
though Maximilian Bray kept up a drawling series of remarks, they fell upon inat-
tentive ears.

'Do you expect them soon?' said Charley at last, somewhat impatiently, for he was
growing tired of his companion's chatter.

'Ya-as, directly,' said Bray, smiling. 'But, mai dear fellow, why didn't you come over and then escort them?'

Charley did not answer; for just then he caught sight of Laura, radiant of face and dress, sweeping along beside Mrs. Bray, who seemed to cut a way through the crowd at the farther part of the great marquee.

'Here they are,' said Bray, drawing Charley along; 'so now you can be out of your misery.'

'What do you mean?' said Charley sharply.

'Bai Jove! how you take a fellow up! Nothing at all—nothing at all!'

Charley frowned slightly, and then suffered himself to be led up to the Elms party, Mrs. Bray smiling upon him sweetly, and Laura favouring him with a look that was meant to bring him to her side.

But Laura's look had not the desired effect; for Charley stayed talking to Mrs. Bray, after just passing the customary compliments to the younger lady.

A frown—no slight one—appeared on Laura's brow; but in a few seconds it was gone, and, walking back a few paces, she stayed by her younger sisters, with whom Charley could see the young lady of the previous day's encounter.

And now he would have followed Laura in the hope of obtaining an introduction, but he was arrested by a stout committee-man.

'Would he kindly step that way for a moment?'

With an exclamation of impatience, the young man followed, to find that his opinion was wanted as to the suitability of the site chosen for the distribution of the prizes.

'But surely you can obtain some one else?' exclaimed Charley.

'Impossible, my dear sir,' was the reply.

So, after two or three unavailing attempts to obtain a substitute, Charley gave in; for the owner of the grounds, upon being asked, declared that a better choice could not have been made; the principal doctor shook his head; while Mr. Onesimus Bray literally turned and fled upon hearing Charley's request. So, with a feeling of something like despair, the elected prize-giver began to cudgel his brains for the verbiage of a speech, telling himself that he should certainly break down and expose himself to the laughter of the assemblage; for the grandees from miles round had made their way to Lexville to patronise the flower-show; and at last, quite in despair, Charley walked hurriedly down one of the alleys of the garden, passing closely

by the Bray party, and making Laura colour with annoyance at what she called his
neglect.

But Charley Vining's perturbed spirit
was not soothed by the anticipated solitude
of the shady alley; for, before he had gone
twenty yards, he saw Max Bray side by
side with the lady who had occupied a
goodly share of his thoughts since the encounter of the previous day.

Their backs were towards him, but it
was quite evident that Mr. Maximilian
Bray was exerting himself to be as agreeable as possible to his companion, though
with what success it was impossible to say.
At all events, Charley Vining turned sharply
round upon his heel, with a strange feeling
of annoyance entirely new pervading his
spirit.

'How absurd!' he muttered to himself.
'What an ass I was to come to a set-out of

this kind! No fellow could be more out of place!'

Turning out of the alley, he made his way, with rapid, business-like steps, on to the lawn, where the rapidly-increasing company were now gathering in knots, and listening to one of Godfrey's finest selections. To an unbiased observer, the thought might have suggested itself that there was as bright a flower-show, and as beautiful a mingling of hues, out there upon the closely-shaven turf, as within the tent; but Charley Vining was just then no impartial spectator; and, though more than one pair of eyes grew brighter as he approached, he saw nothing but two figures slowly issuing from the other end of the alley, where the guelder roses were showering down their vernal snows.

'I should uncommonly like to wring that Max Bray's neck!' said Charley to

himself, as he threw his stalwart form into
a wicker garden-chair, which creaked and
expostulated dismally beneath the weight it
was called upon to bear; and then, indulg-
ing in rather a favourite habit, he lolled
there, muttering and talking to himself—
cross-examining and answering questions
respecting his uneasiness.

But the more he thought, the more un-
easy he grew, and twice over he shifted
his seat to avoid an attack from some conversational friend whom he saw approaching.

'There, this sort of thing won't do!' he
exclaimed at last. 'I'm afraid I'm going
on the pointed-out road rather too fast.
Suppose I take a dose of the Bray family
by way of antidote.'

So, leaving his seat, he strode towards
where he could see Laura's white parasol;
but his intent was baffled by a couple of

committee-men, who literally took him into
custody—their purpose being to give him
divers and sundry explanations respecting
the distribution of the prizes.

CHAPTER VIII.

SHOOTING AN ARROW.

To have seen the company assembled in the Reverend Henry Lingon's grounds upon that bright afternoon, it might have been imagined that for the time being no marring shadow could possibly cross any breast; for, gaze where you would, the eye rested upon bright pleased faces wreathed in smiles, groups, whose aspect was of the happiest, setting off everywhere the Watteau-like landscape. But for all that, there were faces there wearing but a mask, and to more than one present that fête was fraught with *ennui* and disappointment. Toilettes arranged with the greatest care had, in other than the instance hinted at, been without effect; while again, where, in all simplicity, effect had not been sought, attentions had been paid distasteful even to annoyance. The Lexville flower-show had assembled together enough to form a little world of hopes and fears; and, fête-day though it had been, there were aching hearts that night, and tearful eyes moistening more than one pillow—the pillows of those who were young and hopeful still, in spite of their pain, though they were beginning to learn how much bitterness there is amidst the dregs of every cup—dregs to be drained by all in turn, earlier or later, in their little span.

But now the band was silenced for a while, and the company began to cluster around a temporary platform erected for the occasion, where the hero of the day was to distribute to the expectant gardeners the rewards of their care and patience.

Not that there is much to be called
heroic in giving a few premiums for the
best roses, or pansies, or stove-plants; but
if the distributor be young, handsome, disengaged, heir to a baronetcy, and rich, in
many eyes he becomes a hero indeed—a
hero of romance; and bitter as were the
feelings of Charley Vining, who declared to
himself that his speech was blundering,
that he had looked *gauche* and red-faced,
and that any schoolboy could have done
better, there were plenty of hearty plaudits
for him, and more than one bright young
face became suffused with the rapid beating
of its owner's heart, as for a moment she
thought that a glance was directed expressly
at her.

Poor deluded little thing, though! It
was all a mistake; for Charley Vining went
through his business like an automaton, seeing nothing but a simple, half-mourning mus-

lin dress, and a pale sweet face in a lavender
bonnet, which had appeared to him to have
been haunted the whole day long by what
he had once indignantly called 'a tailor's
dummy'—to wit, the exquisite and elabor-
ately-attired form of Maximilian Bray.

But at length the distribution was at
an end, and gardener, amateur, and cottager
had been dismissed. Hot, weary, and glad
to get away, Charley had hurried from the
group of friends and acquaintances by whom
he had been surrounded, when at a short
distance off he espied Laura Bray, and his
heart smote him for his neglect of the
daughter of a family with whom he had
always been very intimate.

'Too bad, 'pon my word!' said Charley
hypocritically, for at the same moment
other thoughts had flashed across his mind.
However, he drew down that mental blind
which people find so convenient wherewith

to shadow the window of their hearts, and
strode across the lawn towards Laura, who
was apparently listening to the conversation of a gentleman of a more fleshy texture
than is general with young men of three- or
four-and-twenty.

'At last!' muttered Laura Bray, as
Charley came smiling up to where she
stood; and now beneath that smile the
feeling of anger and annoyance at what she
had looked upon as his neglect melted
away. True, he owed her no allegiance;
but she had set herself upon receiving his
incense, and the afternoon having passed
with hardly a word, a feeling of disappointment of the most bitter nature had troubled
her: the music had seemed dirge-like, the
brilliant flowers as if strewn with ashes.
At times she was for leaving; but no, she
could not do that. She had darted angry
and reproachful glances at him again and

again, but without effect, and then looked
at him with eyes subdued and tearful, still
in vain: he had seemed almost to avoid
her, and such pains too as she had taken to
make herself worthy of his regard! How
she had bitten her lips till the blood had
nearly started from beneath the bruised
skin! Rage and disappointment had between them shared her breast. Then in a
fit of anger she had commenced quite a
flirtation with Hugh Lingon, the son of
the owner of the grounds, a fat young
gentleman from Cambridge, an ardent cro-
quetist, but rather famed in his set for the
number of times he had been 'ploughed for
smalls.' Hugh Lingon had been delighted,
smiling so much that the great creases in
his fat face almost closed his eyes. He
even went so far as to squeeze Laura's hand,
and to tell her that the cup ought to have
been presented to her as the fairest flower

there; but Charley Vining had not seemed to mind the attentions in the least—he had not even appeared troubled; and at last poor Hugh Lingon was snubbed while uttering some platitude, and sent about his business by the imperious beauty, to make room for Charley Vining, whose pleasant smile chased away all Laura's care.

Of course she must make allowances for him. He had been busy and bothered about the prize-giving, so how could he attend to her? He was different from other men: so frank and straightforward and bold. She had always felt that he must love her; and after what Sir Philip Vining had hinted to papa, and papa had told mamma, and mamma had pinched her arm and told her in a whisper, what was there to prevent her being Lady Vining and the mistress of Blandfield Court?

'At last!' said Laura, and this time

quite aloud, as Charley came up; when, taking his arm, she bestowed upon him a most reproachful glance. 'I declare I thought your friends were to be quite neglected!'

'Neglected? O, I don't know,' said Charley; and then there was a pause.

'Why, you grow quite *distrait!*' said Laura pettishly. 'Why, what can you see to take your attention there?'

She followed his gaze, which was directed towards a seat across the lawn, whereon were her companion of the day before, one of the 'children,' and Max Bray leaning in an attitude over the back.

'Shall we be moving?' said Charley abstractedly.

'O yes, please do!' said Laura. 'I'm dying for want of an ice, or a cup of tea. I've been pestered for the last half-hour by that horrible fat boy!'

'Fat boy!' said Charley wonderingly.

'Yes; you know whom I mean—Hugh Lingon. So glad to have you come and set me free!'

Charley Vining did not say anything; but he led his companion towards the refreshment-tent, carefully avoiding the open lawn, and taking her, nowise unwilling, round by the shady walks where there were but few people, her steps growing slower, and her hand more heavy in its pressure. And still Charley Vining was quiet and thoughtful; but he led his companion to the refreshment-tent, handed the demanded ice, and then sauntered with her towards the lawn, still gay with fashionably-dressed groups.

'Had we not better get in the shade?' said Laura languidly. 'The afternoon sun is quite oppressive.'

'Let's cross over to Max,' said Charley. 'That seems a pleasant shady seat.'

Laura did not speak, but she looked sidewise in his preoccupied countenance, and, evidently piqued at what she considered his indifference, allowed herself to be led across the lawn.

'By the way, Miss Bray,' said Charley suddenly, 'you never introduced me to your lady friend.'

'Lady friend!' said Laura, as if surprised.

'Yes, the fair girl that friend Max there seems so taken with. Is it his *fiancée*?'

Laura Bray's eyes glittered as she bent forward and looked intently in her companion's face; then a tightness seemed to come over the muscles of her countenance, giving her a hard bitter look, as a flash of suspicion crossed her mind. The next moment she smiled; but it was not a pleasant smile, though it displayed two rows of the most brilliantly-white teeth. But, apparently determined upon her course, she increased the pace at which they were walking till they stood in front of the seat where, with a troubled look in her eyes, sat, listening perforce to the doubtless agreeable conversation of Mr. Maximilian Bray, the lady of the railway station, and the companion of Laura in the brougham.

It was with a look almost of malice that, stopping short, Laura fixed her eyes upon Charley Vining, to catch the play of his countenance as, without altering the direction of her glance, she said aloud:

'Miss Bedford, this gentleman has requested to be introduced to you — Mr. Charles Vining.' Then, with mock courtesy, and still devouring each twitch and movement, she continued: 'Mr. Charles Vining—Miss Bedford, *our new governess !'*

CHAPTER IX.

MR. ONESIMUS BRAY led rather an uncomfortable life at home, and more than once
he had confided his troubles to the sympathising ear of Sir Philip Vining. Laura
was given to snubbing him; Max made no
scruple about displaying the contempt in
which he held his parent; while as to Mrs.
Bray, the wife of his bosom, the principal
cause of his suffering from her was the way
in which she sat upon him.

Now it must not be supposed that Mrs.
Bray literally and forcibly did perform any
such act of cruelty; for this was only Mr.
Bray's metaphorical way of speaking in
alluding to the way in which he was kept
down and debarred from having a voice in

his own establishment, the consequence being that he sought for solace and recreation
elsewhere.

Mr. Onesimus Bray was far from being
a poor man; so that if he felt inclined to
indulge in any particular hobby, his banker
never said him ' Nay,' while if Mrs. Bray's
somewhat penurious alarms could be laid
by the promise of profit, she would raise
not the slightest opposition to her husband's projects. At the present time, Mr.
Bray's especial hobby was a model farm, in
which no small sum of money had been
sunk—of course, with a view to profit;
but so far the returns had been *nil*. The
old farmers of the neighbourhood used to
wink and nod their heads together, and
cackle like so many of their own geese at
what they called Mr. Bray's ' fads'—namely,
at his light agricultural carts and wagons;
despising, too, his cows and short-legged

pigs; but, all the same, losing no chance of obtaining a portion of his stock when occasion served.

Moved by a strong desire to possess the finest Southdown sheep in the county, Mr. Bray had purchased a score of the best to be had for money, among which was a snowy-wooled patriarchal ram, as noble-looking a specimen of its kind as ever graced a Roman triumphal procession ere bedewing with its heart's blood the sacrificial altar. Gentle, quiet, and inoffensive, the animal might have been played with by a child before it arrived at Mr. Bray's model farmstead; but having been there confined for a few days in a brick-walled pig-sty, the unfortunate quadruped attracted the notice of the young gentleman whose duty it was to clean knives, boots, and shoes at the Elms, and wait table at dinner, clothed in a jacket glorious with an abun-

dant crop of buttons gracefully arranged
in the outline of a balloon over his padded
chest. It occurred to this young gentleman one afternoon when alone, that a little
playful teasing of the ram might afford him
some safe sport; so fetching a large new
thrum mop from the kitchen, he held it
over the side of the pig-sty, shaking it
fiercely and threateningly at the ram, till
the poor beast answered the challenge of
the—to him—strange enemy by backing as
far as possible, and then running with all
his might at the suddenly-withdrawn mop,
when his head would come with stunning
violence against the bricks, making the wall
quiver again.

The pleasant pastime used to be carried
on very frequently, till most probably, not
from soreness—rams' heads being slightly
thick, and able to suffer even brick walls—
but from disappointment at not being able

to smite its adversary, the ram became changed into a decidedly vicious beast, and, as such, he was turned out into one of Mr. Bray's pleasant meadows.

Now, as it fell upon a day, perfectly innocent of there being any vicious animal in the neighbourhood, Ella Bedford had passed through this very meadow during a walk with her three pupils. The morning was bright and sunshiny, and the sight of a fine snowy-wooled sheep cropping the bright green herbage was not one likely to create alarm. Had it been a cow, or even a calf, it might have been different, and the stiles and footpaths avoided for some other route; for the female eye is a strong magnifier of the bovine race, and we have known ladies refuse to pass through a field containing half-a-dozen calves, which had been magnified, one and all, into bulls of the largest and fiercest character.

There was something delightful to Ella in the sweet repose of the country around. The grass was just springing into its brightest green, gilded here and there with the burnished buttercups, while in every hedgeside 'oxlips and the nodding violet' were blooming; the oaks, too, were beginning to wear their livery of green and gold. The birds sang sweetly as they jerked themselves from spray to spray, while that Sims Reeves of the feathered race—the lark—balanced himself far up in the blue ether, and poured out strain after strain of liquid melody. There was that wondrous elasticity in the air, that power which sets the heart throbbing, and the mind dreaming of something bright, ethereal, ungrasped, but now nearer than ever to the one who drinks in the sweet intoxicating breath of spring.

There was a brightness in Ella's eye, and a slight flush in her cheek, as she

walked on with her pupils, smiling at each
merry conceit, and feeling young herself,
in spite of the age of sorrow that had been
hers.   For a while she forgot the strange
home and the cool treatment she was receiving; the unpleasant attentions, too, of
the hopeful son of the house; the meeting
in the gallery. The wearisome compliments
at the flower-show were set aside; for
—perhaps influenced by the bright morning—Ella's cheek grew still more flushed,
and in spite of herself she dwelt upon the
scene where she pictured two beings addressed by a frank bold horseman; and as
his earnest gaze seemed directed once more
at her, Ella's heart increased its pulsations,
but only to be succeeded by a dull sense of
aching misery, as another picture floated
before her vision, to the exclusion of the
sunny landscape and the glorious spring
verdure.   The sweet liquid trill of the

birds, too, grew dull on her ear; for she seemed once more to see the same earnest gaze fixed upon her face, and then to watch the start of surprise—was it disappointment?—as again Laura Bray's words rang on her ears:

'Miss Bedford, our new governess!'

It was time to cease dreaming, she thought.

Walks must come to an end sooner or later; and a reference to her watch showing Ella Bedford that they would only reach the Elms in time for lunch, they began to retrace their steps. when, to the young girl's horror, she saw that they had been followed by no less a personage than Mr. Maximilian Bray. whose first act upon reaching them was to take his place by Ella's side, and send his sisters on in advance.

But that was not achieved without dif-

ficulty, Miss Nelly turning round sharply
and declining to go.

'I sha'n't go, Max! You only want to
talk sugar to Miss Bedford ; and ma says
you're ever so much too attentive—so there
now!'

Ella's face became like scarlet, and
she increased her pace ; but a whisper
from Max sent Nelly scampering off
after her two sisters—now some distance
in advance—when he turned to the governess.

'Glad I caught up to you, Miss Bedford
—I am, bai Jove! You see, I wanted to
have a few words with you.'

'Mr. Maximilian Bray will, perhaps,
excuse my hurrying on,' said Ella coldly.
'It is nearly lunch-time, and I am obliged
to teach punctuality to my pupils.'

'Bai Jove! ya-as, of course!' said Max.
'But I never get a word with you at home,

and I wanted to set myself right with you about that station matter.'

'If Mr. Bray would be kind enough to forget it, I should be glad,' said Ella quickly.

'Bai Jove! ya-as; but, you see, I can't. You see, it was all a joke so as to introduce myself like. being much struck, you know. Bai Jove. Miss Bedford! I can't tell you how much struck I was with your personal appearance—can't indeed!'

Ella's lip curled with scorn as she slightly bent her head and hurried on.

'Don't walk quite so fast, my dear—Miss Bedford,' he added after a pause. as he saw the start she gave. 'We shall be time enough for lunch, I daresay. Pleasant day, ain't it?'

Ella bent her head again in answer, but still kept on forcing the pace; for the children were two fields ahead, and racing on as quickly as possible.

'Odd, wasn't it, Miss Bedford, that we should have met as we did, and both coming to the same place? Why don't you take my arm? There's nobody looking—this time,' he added.

The hot blood again flushed up in Ella's cheek as she darted an indignant glance at her persecutor; but there was something in Max Bray's composition which must have prevented him from reading aright the signs and tokens of annoyance in others; and, besides, he was so lost in admiration of his own graces and position, that when, as he termed it, he *stooped* to pay attentions to an inferior, every change of countenance was taken to mean modest confusion or delight.

'There, don't hurry so!' he exclaimed, laughing. 'Bai Jove, what a fierce little thing you are! Now, look here: we're quite alone, and I want to talk to you.

There, you needn't look round: the children are half-way home, and we shall be
quite unobserved. Bai Jove! why, what a
prudish little creature you are!'

Ella gave a quick glance round, but only
to find that it was just as Max had said.
There was a sheep feeding in the field,
whose hedges were of the highest; and for
aught she could see to the contrary, there
was no assistance within a mile, while Max
Bray had caught her hand in his, and was
barring the route.

Regularly driven to bay, Ella turned
upon him with flaming face, trying at the
same moment to snatch away her hand,
which, however, he held the tighter, crushing her fingers painfully, though she never
winced.

'Mr. Bray,' she exclaimed, 'do you wish
me to appeal to your father for protection?'

'Of course not!' he drawled. 'But

there now—bai Jove! what is the use of
your putting on all those fine airs and coy
ways? Do you think I'm blind, or don't
understand what they mean? Come now,
just listen to what I say.'

Before Ella could avoid his grasp, he
had thrown one arm round her waist, when
he started back as if stung, for a loud
mocking laugh came from the stile.

'Ha, ha, ha! I thought so! I knew
you wanted to talk sugar to Miss Bedford.'

At the same moment Max and Ella had
seen the merry delighted countenance of
Nelly, who had crept silently back, but now
darted away like a deer.

A cold chill shot through Ella Bedford's
breast, and it was with the greatest difficulty that she could force back the angry
tears as she saw that her future was completely marred at the Elms—how that she
was, as it were, at the mercy of the young

girl placed in her charge, unless she forestalled any tattling by complaining herself
of the treatment to which she had been
subjected.

'There, you needn't mind her!' ex-
claimed Max, who partly read her thoughts.
'I can keep her saucy little tongue quiet.
You need not be afraid.'

'Afraid!' exclaimed Ella indignantly, as
she turned upon the speaker with flashing
eyes, and vainly endeavoured to free the
hand Max had again secured.

'Handsomer every moment, bai Jove!'
exclaimed Max. 'You've no idea how a
little colour becomes you! Now, I just
want to say a few—'

'Are you aware, sir, that this is a cruel
outrage? — one of which no gentleman
would be guilty.'

'Outrage? Nonsense! What stuff you
do talk, my dear! I should have thought

that, after what I said to you at the flower-
show, you would have been a little more
gentle, and not gone flaming out at a poor
fellow like this. You see, I love you to
distraction, Miss Bedford — I do indeed.
Bai Jove, I couldn't have thought that it
was possible for any one to have made such
an impression upon me. Case of love at
first sight — bai Jove, it was! And here
you are so cruel—so hard—so— 'Pon my
soul I hardly know what to call it—I don't,
bai Jove!'

'Mr. Bray,' said Ella passionately, 'every
word that you address to me in this way is
an insult. As the instructor of your sisters, your duty should be to protect, not
outrage my feelings at every encounter.'

She struggled to release her hand, but
vainly. Each moment his grasp grew
firmer, and, like some dove in the claws
of a hawk, she panted to escape. She felt

that it would be cowardly to call for help;
besides, it would be only making a scene in
the event of assistance being near enough
to respond to her appeal; and she had no
wish to figure as an injured heroine or
damsel in distress. Her breast heaved, and
an angry flush suffused her cheeks, while,
in spite of every effort, the great hot tears
of annoyance and misery would force themselves to her eyes. She knew it not—
though she saw the exquisite's gaze fixed
more and more intently upon her—she
knew not how excitement was heightening
the soft beauty of her face, brightening her
eyes, suffusing her countenance with a
warm glow, and lending animation where
sorrow had left all tinged with a sad air of
gloom—an aspect that had settled down
again after the brightness given by the
early part of her walk.

'There now, don't be foolish, and hurt

the poor little white hand! You can't get away, my little birdie; for I've caught you fast. And don't get making those bright eyes all dull and red with tears. I don't like crying—I don't indeed, bai Jove! Now let's walk gently along together. There— that's the way. And now we can talk, and you can listen to what I have to say.'

In spite of her resistance, he drew the young girl's hand through his arm, and held it thus firmly. But to walk on, Ella absolutely refused; and stopping short, she tried to appeal to his feelings.

'Mr. Bray,' she said, 'as a gentleman, I ask you to consider my position. You have already done me irreparable injury in the eyes of your sister; and now by this per-secution you would force me to leave my situation, perhaps with ignominy. I appeal to your feelings—to your honour—to cease this unmanly pursuit.'

' Ah, that's better !' he said mockingly.
' But I'm afraid, my dear, you have a strong
tinge of the romantic in your ideas. I see,
you read too many novels; but you'll come
round in time to my way of thinking, only
don't try on so much of this silly prudish-
ness, my dear. It don't do, you know, because I can see through it. There, now,
don't struggle; only I'm not going to let
you go without something to remember
this meeting by. Now don't be silly!
It's no robbery — only an exchange. I
want that little ring to hang at my watch-
chain, and you can wear this one for my
sake. There !' he exclaimed triumphantly,
as he succeeded in drawing a single gem
pearl ring from her finger and placing one
he drew from his pocket in its place, Ella
the while alternately pale and red with
suppressed anger, for she had vainly looked
around for help; and now forcing back her

tears, and scorning to display any farther
weakness, she took off the ring and dashed
it upon the path.

'What a silly little thing it is!' laughed
Bray, who considered that he was hon-
ouring her with his attentions, however
rough they might be. 'But it's of no
use: you don't go till that ring is on
your darling little finger—you don't, bai
Jove!'

Was there to be no help? A minute before, she would have refused assistance; for
she did not believe that any one professing to be a gentleman would so utterly have
turned a deaf ear to her protestations and
appeals. From some low drink-maddened
ruffian she might have fled in horror, ·
shrieking, perhaps, for help; but here, with
the son of her employers, Ella had believed
that her indignant rejection of the insulting
addresses would have been sufficient to set

her at liberty. She was, then, half stunned as to her mental faculties on finding that her words were mocked at, her appeals disregarded, and even her indignant looks treated as feints and coyness. But then, poor girl, she did not know Maximilian Bray, and that his gross nature was not one that could grasp the character of a good and pure-hearted woman. It was something he could not understand. He measured other natures by his own, and acted accordingly. Once only the thoughts of Ella Bedford flew towards Charles Vining, as if, in spite of herself, they sought in him her natural protector, but only for an instant ; and now, seriously alarmed, she gazed earnestly round for aid. She would have even gladly welcomed the mocking face of Nelly, and have called her to her side. But no, Nelly had hurried away, content and laughing at what she had seen :

and now from the indignant flush, Ella's face began to pale into a look of genuine alarm. But help was at hand.

Still holding tightly by her hand, Max Bray stooped to recover the ring, when, suddenly as a flash of light, a white rushing form seemed to dart through the air, catching Max Bray, as he bent down, right upon the crown of his hat, crushing it over his eyes, and tumbling him over and over, as a fierce 'Ba-a-a-a!' rung upon his astonished ears.

Set free by this unexpected preserver, Ella, panting and alarmed, fled for the stile and climbed it, when, looking back, she saw that she was safe, while Max Bray rose, struggling to free himself from his crusheddown hat; but only for his father's prize Southdown to dart at and roll him over again: when, once more rising to his feet, he ran, frightened and blindfold, as hard as he could across the field in the opposite direction.

Ella saw no more. It did not fall to her lot to see Max Bray make a blind bound—a leap in the dark—from his unseen pursuer, and land in the midst of a dense blackthorn hedge, out of which he struggled, torn of flesh and coat, to free himself from the extinguishing hat, and gaze through the hedge-gap at his assailant, who stood upon the other side shaking his head, and bucking and running forward 'ba-a-a-ing' furiously.

For a few moments Max Bray was speechless with rage and astonishment. To think that he, Maximilian Bray, should have been bowled over, battered, and made to flee ignominiously by a sheep! It was positively awful.

'You — you — you beast! you—you woolly brute!' he stuttered at last. 'I'll

—I'll—bai Jove, I'll shoot you as sure as
you're there!—I will, bai Jove!'

But now the worst of the affair flashed
upon him, making torn clothes, thorns in
the flesh, and battered hat seem as nothing, though these were in his estimation
no trifles; but this was the second time
within the past few days that he had been
wounded in his self-esteem.

'And now there's that confounded coy
jade run home laughing at me—I'm sure
she has!' he muttered. 'Not that there
was anything to laugh at; but never mind:
" Every dog—" My turn will come! But
to be upset like this! And—what? you
won't let me come through!'

There was no doubt about it. The
Southdown was keeping guard at the stile,
and Max Bray, after trying to repair
damages, was glad to make his way back
to the Elms by a circuitous route, and then

to creep in by the side-door unseen, vowing
vengeance the while against those who had
brought him to that pass.

'But I'll make an end of the sheep!' he
exclaimed—'I will, bai Jove!'

CHAPTER X.

MOST persons possessed of feeling will
readily agree that scarcely anything could
be more unpleasant than for a gentleman,
bent upon making himself attractive to a
lady, to meet with such a misfortune as to
be taken, while in a stooping position, for
a defiant beast, and to have to encounter
the full force of a woolly avalanche, or so
much live mutton discharged, as from a
catapult, right upon the crown of his head.
Max Bray was extremely sore afterwards—
sore in person and temper: but the most
extraordinary part of the affair is, that his
head never ached from the fierce blow.   It
would perhaps be invidious to offer re-

marks about thickness, or to make com-
parisons; but certainly for two or three
days after, when he encountered Ella Bedford, Max Bray did wear, in spite of his
effrontery, a decidedly sheepish air. But
not for a longer period. At the end of that
time a great deal of the soreness had worn
off, and he was nearly himself again.

But with Ella Bedford the case was
different. She was hourly awakening to
the fact that hers was to be no pleasant
sojourn at the Elms; and with tearful eyes
she thought of the happy old days at home
before sickness fell upon the little country
vicarage, and then death removed the
simple, good-hearted village clergyman from
his flock, to be followed all too soon by his
mourning wife.

'I have nothing to leave you, my child
—nothing!' were almost the father's last
words. 'Always poor and in delicate

health, I could only keep out of debt. But your mother, help her—be kind to her,' he whispered.

Ella Bedford's help and kindness were only called for during a few months; and then it fell to her lot to seek for some situation where the accomplishments, for the most part taught by her father, might be the means of providing her with a home and some small pittance.

By means of advertising, she had succeeded in obtaining the post of governess at the Elms, and it was while on her way to fill that post that she had encountered the hopeful scion of the house of Bray. It was, then, with a feeling almost of horror that she met him again at the Elms, and her first thought was that she must flee directly—leave the house at once; her next that she ought to relate her adventure to some one. But who would sympathise with her, and rightly view it all? She shrank from harsh loud-voiced Mrs. Bray; and, almost from the first meeting, Laura had seemed to take a dislike to her—one which she made no scruple of displaying—while, as a rule, she tried all she could to show the immeasurable distance she considered that there existed between her and the dependent.

On the day of the sheep encounter, agitated, wounded, and with great difficulty keeping back her tears, Ella hurried on; and had Max Bray's position been one of danger, it is very doubtful whether any assistance would have been rendered him through Ella, so thoroughly was she taken up with her own position. She felt that she must be questioned respecting her charges reaching home alone; they would certainly talk about her staying behind with their brother, and the culminating point would be reached when Miss Nelly declared what she had seen.

Well might the poor girl's heart beat as she hastened on; for it seemed as if, through the persecution of a fop, her prospects in life were to be blighted at the outset. But there's a silver lining to every cloud, it is said; and before Ella had gone half a mile, to her great joy she saw Nelly seated with her sisters by a bank, gathering wild flowers, and then tossing them away.

Fortune favoured her too when they reached the Elms: luncheon—the children's dinner—had been put back for half an hour because Mr. Maximilian had not returned.

'Mr. Maximilian' did not show himself at all at table that day, and, glad of the respite, Ella sought her bedroom directly after, to think over the past, and try and decide what ought to be her course under the circumstances. What would she not

have given for the loving counsel of some
gentle, true-hearted woman! But she felt
that she was quite alone—alone in the vast
weary world; and as such thoughts sprang
up came the recollection of the happy
bygone, sweeping all before it; and at last,
unable to bear up any longer, she sank
upon her knees by the bedside, weeping
and sobbing as if her poor torn heart would
break.

She struggled hard to keep the tears
back, but in vain now—they would come,
and with them fierce hysterical sobs, such
as had never burst before from her breast.
Then would come a cessation, as she asked
herself whether she ought not to acquaint
Mrs. Bray with her son's behaviour?—or
would it be making too much of the
affair? Then she reviewed her own conduct, and tried to find in it some flaw—some
want of reserve which had brought upon

her the insults to which she had been subjected. But, as might be expected, the
search was vain, and once more she bowed
down her head and sobbed bitterly for the
happy past, the painful present, and the
dreary future.

It was in the midst of her passionate
outbursts that she suddenly felt some one
kneel beside her, and through her tears she
saw, with wonder, the friendly and weeping
face of Nelly, who had crept unperceived
into the room.

'O, Miss Bedford! Dear, dear Miss
Bedford, please don't—don't!' sobbed the
girl, as, throwing her long thin arms round
Ella, she drew her face to her own hard
bony breast, soothing, kissing, and fondling
her tenderly, as might a mother. 'Please
—please don't cry so, or you'll break my
heart; for, though you don't think it, I do
love you so—so much! You're so gentle,

and kind, and wise, and beautiful, that—
that—that—O, and you're crying more
than ever!'

Poor Nelly burst out almost into a
howl of grief as she spoke; but, like her
words, it was genuine, and as she pressed
her rough sympathies upon her weeping
governess, Ella's sobs grew less laboured,
and she clung convulsively to the slight
form at her side.

'There — there — there!' half sobbed
Nelly. 'Try not to cry, dear; do please
try, dear Miss Bedford; for indeed, indeed
it does hurt me so! You made me to love
you, and I can't bear to see you like this!'

So energetic, indeed, was Nelly's grief,
that, as she spoke, she kicked out behind,
overturning a bedroom chair; but it passed
unnoticed.

'They say I'm a child; but I'm not,
you know!' she said half passionately. 'I'm

sixteen nearly, and I can see as well as
other people. Yes, and feel too! I'm not
a child; and if Laury raps my knuckles
again, I'll bite her, see if I don't! But I
know what you're crying about, Miss Bedford, and I saw you wanted to cry all din-
ner-time, only you couldn't; it's about
Max; and you thought I should tell that
he put his arm round your waist. But I
sha'n't—no, not never to a single soul, if
they put me in the rack! He's a donkey,
Max is, and a disagreeable, stupid, cox-
comby, stubborn, bubble-headed donkey,
that he is! I saw him kiss Miss Twentyman, who used to be our governess, and
she slapped his face—and serve him right
too, a donkey, to want to kiss anybody—
such stupid silly nonsense! It's quite right
enough for girls and women to kiss; but
for a man—pah! I don't believe Max was
ever meant to be anything but a girl,

though; and I told him so once, and he boxed my ears, and I threw the butter-plate at him, and the butter stuck in his whiskers, and it was such fun I forgot to cry, though he did hurt me ever so. But I'm not a child, Miss Bedford, and I do love you ever so much, and I'll never say a single word about you and Max; and if he ever bothers you again, you say to him, " How's Miss Brown?" and he'll colour up, and be as cross as can be. I often say it to make him cross. He used to go to see her, and she wouldn't have him because she said he was such a muff, and she married Major Tompkins instead. But it does make him cross—and serve him right too, a nasty donkey! Why, if he'd held my hand like he did yours to-day, I'd have pinched him, and nipped him, and bitten him, that I would! He sha'n't never send me away any more, though; I shall always stop with

you, and take care of you, if you'll love me
very much ; and I will work so hard—so
jolly hard—with my studies, Miss Bedford,
I will indeed ; for I'm so behindhand, and
it was all through Miss Twentyman being
such a cross old frump ! But you needn't
be afraid of me, dear; for I'm not a child,
am I ?'

As Nelly Bray had talked on, fondling
her to whom she clung the while, Ella's
sobs had grown less frequent, and at last,
as she listened to the gaunt overgrown
girl's well-meaning, half-childish, half-wo-
manly words, she smiled upon her through
her tears; for her heart felt lighter, and
there was relief, too, in the knowledge that
Nelly was indeed enough of a true-hearted
woman to read Max Bray's conduct in the
right light, and to act accordingly.

'You darling dear sweet love of a governess !' cried Nelly rapturously, as she saw

the smile; and clinging to her neck, she showered down more kisses than were, perhaps, quite pleasant to the recipient. 'You will trust me, won't you?'

'I will indeed, dear,' said Ella softly.

'And you won't fidget?'

'No,' said Ella.

'And now—that's right; wipe your eyes and sit down—and now you must talk to me, and take care of me. But you are not cross because I came up without leave?'

'Indeed, no,' said Ella sadly. 'I thought I was without a friend, and you came just at that time.'

'No, no, you mustn't say that,' said Nelly, 'because I am not old and sensible enough to be your friend. But it hurt me to see you in such trouble, and I was obliged to come; and now you won't be miserable any more; and you mustn't take any notice if Laury is disagreeable—a nasty thing!

flirting all day long with my—with Mr.
Hugh Lingon,' she said, colouring. 'But
there, I'm not ashamed: Hugh Lingon is
my lover, and has been ever since he was
fourteen and I was six—when he used to
give me sweets, and I loved him, and used
to say he was so nice and fat to pinch!
And Laury was flirting with him all that
afternoon at the show, when Max would
hang about—a great stupid!—when I wanted
to explain things; for you know she was
flirting with Hugh because that dear old
Charley Vining wouldn't take any notice
of her. He is such a dear nice fellow!
But I do not love *him*, you know, only
like him; and he likes me ever so much.
He told me so one day, and gave me half-
a-crown to spend in sweets—wasn't it kind
of him? He'll often carry a basket of
strawberries or grapes over for me and the
girls, or fill his pockets with apples and

pears for us; when, as for old Max, he'd
faint at the very sight of a basket, let alone
carry it! You will like Charley. He *is*
nice! Laury loves him awful—talks about
him in her sleep! But I do not think he
cares for her,—and no wonder! But I
say, Miss Bedford, how nice and soft your
hand is! and, I say, what a little one!
Why, mine's twice as big!'

Ella smiled, and went on smoothing the
girl's rough hair, but hardly heeding what
she said—only catching a word here and
there.

'I shouldn't never love Charley Vining,'
said Nelly, whose grammar was exceedingly
loose, 'but I should always like him; and
if I don't marry Hugh Lingon, I mean to
be an old maid, and wear stiff caps and
pinners, and then— You're beginning to
cry again, and it's too bad, after all this
comforting up!'

'No, indeed, my child,' said Ella, rousing herself. 'I was only thinking that
when things are at the blackest some little
ray of hope will peep out to light our
paths.'

'I say,' said Nelly, 'is that poetry?'

'No,' said Ella, smiling sadly.

'Ah, I thought it was,' said Nelly.
'But then I'm so ignorant and stupid!
Mamma says I'm fit for nothing, and I suppose she's right! But there, I'm making
you tired with my talking, and I won't say
another word; only don't you fidget about
Max—only snub him well; and I wouldn't
tell pa or ma, because it might make mischief.'

Hanging as it were in the balance, Ella
allowed the advice of the child-woman at
her side to have effect, and determined to
say nothing—to make no complaints, trusting to her own firmness to keep her perse-

cutor in his place until his visit was at an
end. It was, perhaps, a weak resolve: but
who is there that always takes the better
of two roads? It was, however, her decision—her choice of way—one which led
through a cloud of sorrow, misery, and despair so dense, that in after time poor Ella
often asked herself was there to be no
turning, no byway that should lead once
again, if but for a few hours, into the joyous sunshine of life?

CHAPTER XI.

'Bai Jove, seems a strange thing!' said Max Bray at breakfast-time, about a week after the events recorded in the last chapter—'seems a strange thing you women can't settle anything without showing your teeth!'

'You women, indeed! Max, how can you talk so vulgarly!' exclaimed Laura.

And then there was silence, for Ella Bedford entered the breakfast-room with her charges.

Strange or not, there had been something more than a few words that morning in the breakfast-room between Mrs. Bray and her daughter, concerning a croquet-party to come off that afternoon upon the

Elms lawn. As for Mr. Bray, he had taken
no part in the discussion, ' shutting-up'—to
use his son's words — ' like an old gingham
umbrella, bai Jove!"

However, hostilities ceased upon the
appearance of Ella with the children; and
Mrs. Bray, after shrieking for the tea-
caddy, sat down to the urn, and the morning meal commenced.

' Of course, mamma,' said Laura suddenly, ' you won't think of having the children on the lawn?'

' O, I daresay, miss!" cried Nelly, firing
up. ' Just as if we're to be set aside when
there's anything going on! Charley Vining
says I play croquet just twice as well as
you can; and I know he's coming to-day
on purpose to see me!' she added maliciously.

Mr. Bray shook his head at her, and
Ella slightly raised one finger; but as she

made a rule of never correcting her charges when father or mother was present, she did not speak.

'Hold your tongue, you pert child!' exclaimed Laura, with a toss of the head. 'You'll let Miss Bedford keep them in the schoolroom, of course, mamma?'

'Indeed, I don't see why they should not have a game as well as their sister!' shrieked Mrs. Bray, from behind the urn; for after the hostilities of that morning mamma would not budge an inch.

The breakfast ended, Nelly ran round to give Mrs. Bray a sounding kiss, and then danced after her sisters and their governess into the schoolroom.

'There, hooray! Beaten her!' shouted Nelly, clapping her hands. 'I knew what she meant, Miss Bedford. She didn't want you to be on the lawn and come and play; and now she's beaten, and serve her right too! She's afraid Charley Vining will take more notice of you than he does of her, and I shall tell him.'

'My dear Nelly!' exclaimed Ella, with a look of pain on her countenance; when her wild young charge dropped demurely into a seat, and began to devour French irregular verbs at a tremendous rate, working at them thoroughly hard, and, having a very retentive memory, making some progress.

These were Ella's happiest moments; for, in spite of their roughness, the three girls in her charge, one and all, evinced a liking for her; and save at times, when she broke out into a thorough childish fit, Nelly grew hourly more and more womanly under her care. But Ella was somewhat troubled respecting the afternoon's meeting, and would gladly have spent the time in solitude, for it was plain enough that she was to be present solely out of opposition to Laura; and in spite of all her efforts, it seemed that she was to grow daily more distasteful to the dark beauty, who openly showed her dislike before Ella had been in the house a week.

However, the schoolroom studies made very little progress that morning; for before long Mrs. Bray entered to give orders respecting dress, sending Nelly into ecstasies as she cast her book aside; and at three o'clock that afternoon, as Laura swept across the lawn to meet some of the coming guests, there was a look of annoyance upon her countenance that was ill-concealed by the smile she wore.

'So absurd!' she had just found time to say to Mrs. Bray, 'bringing those children and their governess out upon the croquet-ground as if on purpose to annoy people, who are made to give way to humour their schoolroom whims!'

Mrs. Bray's reply was a toss of the head, as she turned off to meet her hopeful son Max, who, after pains that deserved a better recompense, now made his appearance dressed for the occasion.

'Just in time, bai Jove!' he drawled; and then he started slightly, for, making a survey of the lawn, he suddenly became aware that Ella Bedford was seated within a few yards with her pupils. 'O, here's Miss Bedford!' he exclaimed; 'and, let's see, there's Laura; and who are those with her? O, the Ellis people. They don't play. I want to make up a set at once—want another gentleman. Why, there's Charley Vining just coming out of the stable-yard; rode over, I suppose. Perhaps he'll play.'

Ella shrank back, and sent an appealing look towards Mrs. Bray; but as Max had said Miss Bedford was to play, there was no appeal.

'Perhaps Miss Nelly here would like to take my place?' said Ella.

'O, dear me, no, Miss Bedford! Mr. Maximilian selected you as one of the set, and I should not like him to be disappointed,' said Mamma Bray.

'You'll play, Vining?' drawled Max.

'Well, no; I don't care about it,' said Charley good-humouredly. 'I'll make room for some one else.'

'Ya-a-as, but we haven't enough without you,' said Max. 'You might take a mallet, you know, till some one else comes.'

'O, very good,' said Charley, who had just caught sight of Ella with a mallet in her hand. 'I'm ready.'

'Then we'll have a game at once before any one else comes. Now then, Laura, here's Charley Vining breaking his heart because you don't come and play on his side.

I daresay, though, Miss Bedford and I can get the better of you.'

But Max Bray's arrangement for a snug *parti* of four was upset by fresh arrivals— Hugh Lingon, looking very stout, pink, and warm, with a couple of sisters, both stouter, pinker, and warmer, and a very slim young curate from a neighbouring village, arriving just at the same time.

Then followed a little manœuvring and arranging; but in spite of brother and sister playing into each other's hands, the game commenced with Max Bray upon the same side as Laura, one of the stout Miss Lingons, and the slim curate; while Charley Vining had Ella under his wing.

Croquet is a very nice amusement : not that there is much in the game itself, which is, if anything, rather tame; but it serves as a means for bringing people together—

as a vehicle for chatting, flirting, and above
all, carrying off the *ennui* so fond of making its way into social fashionable life.
You can help the trusting friend so nicely
through hoop after hoop, receiving all the
while such prettily-spoken thanks and such
sweet smiles; there is such a fine opportunity too, whilst assuming the leadership and
directing, for enabling the young lady to
properly hold her mallet for the next blow
—arranging the little fingers, and pressing
them inadvertently more tightly to the stick;
and we have known very enthusiastic ama-
teurs go so far as to kneel down before a
lady, and raise one delicate *bottine*, placing
it on the player's ball, and holding it firmly
while the enemy is croque'd. *Apropos*
of enemies, too, how they can be pun-
ished! How a rival can be ignominiously
driven here and there, and into all sorts of
uncomfortable places—under bushes and

behind trees, wired and pegged, and treated in the most cruel manner!

And so it was at the Elms croquet party. Looking black almost as night, Laura struck at the balls viciously—a prime new set of Jaques's best—chipping the edge of her mallet, bruising the balls, and driving Ella Bedford's 'No. 1, blue,' at times right off the croquet-ground. Not that it mattered in the least; for in spite of his self-depreciation, Charley Vining was an admirable player, making long shots, and fetching up Ella's unfortunate ball, taking it with him through hoop after hoop, till Laura's eyes flashed, and Max declared, 'bai Jove!' he never saw anything like it; when Charley would catch a glimpse of Ella's troubled look, recollect himself, and perform the same acts of kindness for the plump Miss Lingon, to receive in return numberless 'O, thank you's!' and 'O, how

clever's!' and 'So much obliged, Mr. Vining!' while 'that governess,' as Laura called
her, never once uttered a word of thanks.
As for Hugh Lingon, he was always no-
where; and as he missed his aim again and
again, he grew more and more divided in
his opinions.

First he declared that the ground was
not level; but seeing the good strokes made
by others, he retracted that observation,
and waited awhile.

'I don't think my ball is quite round,
Vining,' he exclaimed, after another bad
stroke.

'Pooh! nonsense!' laughed Charley.
'You didn't try; it was because you didn't
want to hit Miss Bray.'

'No—no! 'Pon my word, no—'pon my
word!' exclaimed Hugh, protesting as he
grew more and more pink.

'Did his best, I'd swear—bai Jove, he

did!' drawled Max, playing, and sending poor Lingon off the ground.

Then, after a time, Lingon had his turn once more.

'It's not the ball, it's this mallet—it is indeed!' he exclaimed, after an atrocious blow. 'Just you look here, Vining: the handle's all on one side.'

'Never mind! Try again, my boy,' laughed Charley; and soon after he had to bring both his lady partners up again to their hoop, sending Laura's ball away to make room for them, and on the whole treating it rather harshly, Laura's eyes flashing the while with vexation.

'I like croquet for some things,' said Laura's partner, the thin curate, after vainly trying to render her a service; 'but it's a very unchristian-like sort of game—one seems to give all one's love to one's friends, and to keep none for one's enemies.'

'O, come, I say,' laughed Charley, who seemed to be in high spirits. 'Here's Mr. Louther talking about love to Miss Bray!'

'Indeed, I assure you—' exclaimed the curate.

'But I distinctly heard the word,' laughed Charley.

'Was that meant for a witticism?' sneered Laura.

'Wit? no!' said Charley good-humouredly. 'I never go in for that sort of thing.'

'Bai Jove, Vining! why don't you attend to the ga-a-a-me?' drawled Max, who was suffering from too much of the second Miss Lingon—a young lady who looked upon him as an Adonis.

'Not my turn,' said Charley.

'Yes, yes!' said Hugh Lingon innocently. 'Miss Bedford wants you to help her along!

'Of course,' sneered Laura. 'Such impudence!'

But Charley did not hear her words; for he was already half way towards poor Ella, who seemed to shrink from him as he approached, and watched with a troubled breast the efforts he made upon her behalf.

'Now it's my turn again,' said Hugh. 'Now just give me your advice here, Vining. What ought I to do?'

Charley interrupted a remark he was making to Ella Bedford, and pointed out the most advantageous play, when Hugh Lingon raised his mallet, the blow fell, and —he missed.

'Now, did you ever see anything like that?' he exclaimed, appealing to the company.

'Yes, often!' laughed Charley.

'But what can be the reason?' exclaimed Lingon.

'Why, bai Jove! it's because you're such a muff, Lingon, bai Jove!' exclaimed Max.

'I am—I know I am!' said Lingon good-humouredly. 'But, you know, I can't help it—can't indeed!'

The game went on with varying interest, Charley in the intervals trying to engage Ella in conversation ; but only to find her retiring, almost distant, as from time to time she caught sight of a pair of fierce eyes bent upon her from beneath Laura's frowning brows. But there was a sweetness of disposition beaming from Ella's troubled countenance, and the tokens of a rare intellect in her few words—spoken to endeavour to direct him to seek for others with more conversational power, but with precisely the contrary effect—that seemed to rouse in Sir Philip Vining's son feelings altogether new. He found himself dwelling upon every word, every sweet and musical tone, drinking in each troubled, trembling look, and listening with ill-concealed eagerness even for the words spoken to others.

'Bai Jove!' exclaimed Max at length, angrily to his sister, 'what's the matter with that Charley Vining?'

'Don't ask me!' cried Laura pettishly, as she turned from him to listen to and then to snub the slim curate, who, after ten minutes' consideration, had worked up and delivered a compliment.

Once only did Ella trust herself to look at Charley, taking in, though, with that glance the open-countenanced, happy English face of the young man, but shrinking within herself the next instant as she seemed to feel the bold, open, but still respectfully-admiring glance directed at her.

Two other croquet sets had been made upon the great lawn; and, taking the first opportunity, Ella had given up her mallet into other hands—an act, to Laura's great disgust, imitated by Charley Vining, who, however, found no opportunity for again approaching Ella Bedford until the hour of dinner was announced, when, the major portion of the croquet-players having departed, the remainder—the invited few—met in the drawing-room.

CHAPTER XII.

CROSS UPON CROSS.

' WILL you take down Miss Bedford, Max ?'
said Mrs. Bray, according to instructions
from her son, who, however, was not present, his toilet having detained him; and,
therefore, trembling Ella fell to the lot of
Charley Vining, whom, she knew not why,
she seemed to fear now as much as she did
Max Bray.

And yet she could not but own that he
was only frank, cordial, and gentlemanly.
Only! Was that all? She dared not answer
that question. Neither could he answer sundry questions put by his own conscience, as
from time to time he encountered angry,
reproachful glances from the woman who

sat opposite, but to whom, whatever might have been assumed, he had never uttered a word that could be construed into one of love.

Somehow or another, during that dinner, Sir Philip's words would keep repeating themselves to Charley, and at last he found himself muttering: 'Shut myself out from an Eden—from an Eden!' while, when the ladies rose, and the door had closed upon the last rustling silk, a cloud appeared to have come over the scene, and he sat listening impatiently to the drawl of Max, and the agricultural converse of Mr. Bray.

It was with alacrity, then, that Charley left the table, when, upon reaching the drawing-room, he found Laura hovering in a paradise of musical R's, as she sat at the piano, rolling them out in an Italian bravura song, whose pages, for fear that he should be forestalled by Charley Vining, Hugh Lingon rushed to turn over.

'Now Miss Bedford will sing us something,' shrieked Mrs. Bray; and not daring to decline, Ella rose and walked to the piano, taking up a song from the canterbury. But her hands trembled as a shadow seemed to be cast upon her; and without daring to look, she knew that Charley Vining was at her side, ready to turn over the leaves.

'If he would only go!' she thought; and then she commenced with tremulous voice a sweet and plaintive ballad, breathing of home and the past, when, living as it were in the sweet strain, her voice increased in volume and pathos, the almost wild expression thrilling through her hearers, till towards the end of the last verse, when forgetting even Vining's presence in the recollections evoked, Ella was brought back to the present with a start, as one single hot tear-drop fell upon her outstretched hand.

How she finished that song she never knew, nor yet how she concealed her painful agitation; but her next recollection was of being in the conservatory with Charley Vining, alone, and with his deep-toned voice seeming to breathe only for her ear.

'You must think it weak and childish,' he said softly; 'but I could not help it,' he added simply. 'Perhaps I am, after all, only an overgrown boy; but that was my dear mother's favourite song—one which I have often listened to; and as you sung to-night, the old past seemed to come back almost painfully. But I need not fear that you will ridicule me.'

'Indeed, no!' said Ella softly. 'I can only regret that I gave you pain.'

'Pain! No, it was not pain,' said Charley musingly. 'I cannot explain the feeling. I am a great believer in the power of music; and had we been alone, I might have asked you to repeat the strain. I am only too glad, though, that my poor father was not here.'

There was a pause for quite a minute— one which, finding how her companion had been moved, Ella almost feared to break; when seeing him start back, as it were, into the present and its duties, she made a movement as if to return.

'But one minute, Miss Bedford,' said Charley. 'You admire flowers, I see. Look at the metallic, silvery appearance of these leaves.'

'Pray excuse me, Mr. Vining,' said Ella quietly, 'but I wish to return to the drawing-room.'

'Yes—yes—certainly!' exclaimed Charley. 'But one moment: I have something to say to you.'

'Mr. Vining is mistaken,' said Ella coldly; 'he forgets that I am not a visitor or friend of the family. Pray allow me to return!'

'Of course—yes!' said Charley. 'But indeed I have something to say, Miss Bedford. Look here!'

He drew the little gold cross from his pocket, and held it up in the soft twilight shed by the coloured lamps, when his companion uttered a cry of joy.

'I have grieved so for its loss!' she exclaimed. 'You found it?'

'Yes; beneath that tree where you were taking refuge from the rain. I know it was my duty to have returned it sooner; but I wished to place it in your hands myself.'

'O, thank you—I am so grateful!' exclaimed Ella, hardly noticing the *empresse-ment* with which he spoke.

'I wished, too,' said Charley, speaking softly and deeply, 'for some reward for what I have done.'

'Reward?' ejaculated Ella.

'Surely, yes,' said Charley, laying his hand upon the tiny glove resting upon his arm. 'You would accord that to the poorest lout who had been the lucky finder.'

'Reward, Mr. Vining?' stammered Ella.

'Yes!' exclaimed Charley, his rich deep voice growing softer as he spoke. 'And but for those words upon the reverse side, I would have kept the cross as an emblem of my hope. I, too, had a mother who is but a memory now. But you will grant me what I ask?'

'Mr. Vining,' said Ella gravely, but unable to conceal her agitation, 'will you kindly lead me back to the drawing-room?

I thank you for restoring me the cross, which I had never hoped to see again.'

She held out her hand, and the little ornament was immediately placed within her palm.

'You see,' said Charley, 'I trust to your honour. I am defenceless now, but you will give me my guerdon?'

'Reward?' said Ella again.

'Yes,' said Charley eagerly; 'I do not ask much. That rose that you have worn the evening through: give me that—I ask no more.'

'Mr. Vining,' said the agitated girl, 'I am poor and friendless, and here as a dependent. I say thus much, since I believe you to be a gentleman. You would not wilfully injure me, I am sure; but this prolonged absence may give umbrage to my employers. Once more, pray lead me back!'

Charley was moved by the appeal, and he turned on the instant.

'But you will give me that simple flower?' he said.

'Mr. Vining,' said Ella with dignity, 'would you have me lose my self-respect? I thank you for the service — indeed I am most grateful—but I cannot accede to your request.'

'I had hoped that I might be looked on as a friend,' said Charley gloomily, as he once more arrested his companion's steps; 'but there, I suppose if it had been— Pish! forgive me, pray!' he exclaimed. 'How weak and contemptible I am! Miss Bedford, I am quite ashamed to have spoken so. But tell me that you forgive me, and—'

'Is Miss Bedford so mortally offended?' said a voice close at their side. 'I have no doubt we can manage to obtain her for-giveness for you, Mr. Vining. But not to-night, as there will not be time.—Nelly wants you in the schoolroom, Miss Bedford, and then, as it is late, perhaps you had better not return to the drawing-room this evening.'

Ella Bedford started, as, with flashing, angry eyes, Laura Bray stepped forward from behind the thick foliage of an orange-tree, and then, without a word—for she could not have spoken, so bitter, so cruel were the tones, and so deep the sting— Ella glided from the conservatory, leaving Laura face to face with Charley.

'I am sorry to have interrupted so pleasant a tête-à-tête!' exclaimed Laura tauntingly.

There was no answer. Charley merely leaned against the open window, and gazed out upon the starry night; for he could not trust himself to speak, since every humiliat-

ing word addressed to his late companion
had seemed to cut into his own heart; and
had he spoken, it would have been with
some hot angry words, of which he would
afterwards have repented.

'Had I known that Mr. Charles Vining
was so pleasantly engaged, I would not
have come,' said Laura again bitterly, and
with reproach in every tone of her voice.

Again angry words were on Charley's
lips; but for the sake of her who had left
him he crushed them down, as he stood
listening to the impatient foot of the angry
girl beating the tiled floor, and seemed to
feel her eyes burning him as they literally
flashed with suppressed rage.

'Perhaps now that Mr. Vining is disengaged he will lead me back to the drawing-room, as it might be painful to his feelings for people afterwards to make remarks
upon our absence.'

Charley started at this, and made a movement as if to offer his arm; but the remembrance of the cruel insult to the dependent yet rankled in his breast, and he seemed to shrink from the angry woman as from something that he loathed.

Laura saw it, and a sob of rage, disappointment, and passion combined burst from her breast. But even then, if he had made but one sign, she would have softened and thrown herself weeping upon his breast, reproaching, upbraiding, but loving still, and ready to forgive and forget all the past. But Charles Vining was touched to the quick, and, in spite of his calm unmoved aspect, he was hot with passion, wishing in his heart that Max had been the offender, that he might have quenched his rage by shaking him till those white teeth of his chattered again. Then came, though, the thought of Ella Bedford and her position.

If he was cold and distant to Laura, would she not visit it upon that defenceless girl? Then he told himself she could behave with no greater cruelty, humiliate her no more, and he felt that he could not play the hypocrite. His growing dislike for Laura Bray was fast becoming a feeling of hatred, and facing her for a moment, he was about to leave the conservatory alone; but no, the gentlemanly courtesy came back—he could not be guilty of rudeness even to the woman he despised; and without a word, he offered his arm, and prepared to lead her back to the drawing-room.

For a moment Laura made as if to take the proffered arm; but at that moment she caught sight of Charley's frowning, angry face, when, with a cry of passionate grief, she darted past him, and the next instant he saw her cross the hall and hurry upstairs.

'Hyar—hyar, Vining, mai dear fellow, where are you?' cried a drawling voice from the other end of the conservatory.

'Confound it all!' ejaculated Charley, waking as it were into action at the tones of that voice, when with a bound he leaped from the window out on to the lawn, thrust out his Gibus hat, crushed it down again upon his head, and set off with long strides in the direction of the Court.

CHAPTER XIII.

THE CLEARING OF A DOUBT.

'My dear boy, yes—of course I will; and we'll have a nice affair of it! Edgington's people shall fit up a tent and a kiosk, and we'll try and do the thing nicely. You're giving me great pleasure in this, Charley— you are indeed!'

'Am I, father?' said Charley, whose heart smote him as he spoke, telling himself the while that he was deceiving the generous old man, with whom he had hitherto been open as the day.

'Yes, my dear boy—yes, of course you are! It's just what I wanted, Charley, to see you a little more inclined for society. You'll have quite a large party, of course?'

'Well, no, father,' said Charley; 'I think not. Your large affairs are never so successful as the small ones.'

'Just so, my dear boy; I think you are right. Well, have it as you please, precisely, only give your orders. Slave of the lamp, you know, Charley—slave of the lamp: what shall I do first?'

'Well, dad,' said Charley, flushing slightly, 'I thought, perhaps, you wouldn't mind doing a little of the inviting for me.'

'Of course not, my dear boy. Whom shall I ask first?'

'Well, suppose you see the Brays,' said Charley, whose face certainly wore a deeper hue than usual.

'To be sure, Charley!' said the old gentleman, smiling.

'They've been very kind, and asked me there several times, so you'll ask them all?'

'Decidedly!' said the old gentleman.

'We must have Max,' said Charley; 'for he keeps hanging about here still.'

'O, of course!' said Sir Philip.

'And Laura, I suppose,' said Charley, feeling more and more conscience-stricken.

'By all means, my dear boy!' laughed the father.

'And then there are the three girls, *and the governess*,' said Charley.

'Should you ask them?' said Sir Philip.

'O yes, decidedly!' said Charley. 'I'm very fond of that second girl, Nelly; she's only a child, but there's something nice and frank and open about her. She will be sure to make up for the unpleasantry of having Max.'

'Very good, Charley—very good!' said Sir Philip.

'I wouldn't be put off with any of them,' said Charley, in a curious hesitating way. 'Perhaps they'll say that they had better

not all come; but they can't refuse you
anything, so insist upon them bringing the
children and Miss Bedford.'

'Miss who?' said Sir Philip.

'Miss Bedford — the governess,' said
Charley, who coughed as if something had
made him husky. 'I particularly wish for
them all to come.'

'It shall be just as you like, my dear
boy,' said Sir Philip gaily; 'only let's do
the thing well, and not let them go away
and find fault afterwards.'

Charley Vining left his father ill at ease
and dissatisfied, for he felt that he was deceiving the old man; but, like many more,
he crushed down the obtrusive thoughts,
and, going round to the stable, he mounted
his mare as soon as it could be got ready,
and rode slowly and thoughtfully away.

'What's come to the young governor?'
said one of the stablemen.

' O, the old game !' said another. ' He's been betting heavy on the Derby, and lost, and the old gentleman won't pay his debts. I shouldn't be at all surprised if as soon as he comes in for the place, he'll make the money fly.'

' Don't think it's that,' said the other. ' But he never takes a bit of notice of his 'orses now; if they look well, they do, and if they don't look well, they don't; but he's never got a word to say about them. There's something wrong, safe.'

There was a good deal of truth in the remarks of the servants; for the Charley Vining of the present was certainly not the Charley Vining of a month before. Since the night of the croquet-party he had several times met Laura Bray, who, like himself, had endeavoured to ignore entirely their encounter in the conservatory, speaking in the most friendly manner, and en-

deavouring to the best of her ability to bring
Charley more to her side. In fact, so completely was the past evaded, that Charley
called several times, meeting a warmer welcome at every visit; but not once did he
encounter Ella. He was very little more
fortunate during his rides: once he pressed
forward his horse upon seeing her at some
distance down a lane with the 'children;'
but suddenly Max Bray made his appearance, as if by magic, and fixing upon
him, kept by his side for quite an hour;
another time Max was walking with his
sisters and their governess; while upon
a third occasion Max was coming in the
other direction, as if purposely to meet
them, and as Charley rode away his brow
grew dark, and he asked himself what it
meant.

In fact, watch as carefully as he would
for a meeting, his efforts seemed in vain;

while the more he was disappointed, the more eager he became.

It was upon one of these occasions that he had drawn up his horse by a hedge-side, gazing angrily after the distant party, consisting of Ella, two of the children, and Max, when, angry and disappointed, he was considering whether he should canter up after them or turn back.

'Why should I bother myself?' he muttered. 'If she likes that donkey dangling after her, I'm quite convinced that she would not approve of rough unpolished me. I'll give up. Max shall have the field to himself, and I'll go back and ask the governor to let me live in peace. I've only been making a mistake, and neglecting everything for the sake of a pleasant-looking face. Hallo!'

'Ha, ha, ha!' rang out a merry laugh.

'Look at Sir Dismal, pausing thoughtfully beneath the trees.'

Charley looked up, to see peering down upon him, from between the bushes on the high bank, the bright merry face of Nelly, with her hair tangled, her straw hat bent of brim, and a general aspect about her hot face and tumbled clothes of having been tearing through a wood.

'What, my little dryad!' laughed out Charley, brightening in an instant. 'How is the little wood-nymph?'

'O, so jolly hot and tired, Charley! I've cut away from them, run up the bank, and scampered through Bosky Dell, and tore my dress ever so many times. But I wasn't going to stay; at least, I ought to have stayed,' she added thoughtfully, 'but I felt as if I couldn't, for old Max would have made me ill—he would, bai Jove!' she laughed, mocking her bro-

ther's drawl with an accuracy which delighted Charley.

'Been having a walk?' he said.

'Walk, yes,' exclaimed Nelly; 'and one
can't stir without stupid old Max coming
boring after us, bothering Miss Bedford to
death with his drawling nonsense. She
hates him, and he will follow us about,
because he has grown so fond of his little
sisters. But, I say, Charley Vining, do give
me—no, not give, lend me sixpence to buy
some sweets. We spent every halfpenny, and
it isn't pocket-money till to-morrow night.'

'I never give money to beggars at the
roadside,' laughed Charley, who seemed
somehow to be brightening up under his
young friend's revelations.

'Now don't be a nuisance,' laughed
Nelly, 'or I'll tease you. I know why you
were looking down the lane so miserably;
it was because Max was along with—'

'Hold your tongue, do, you saucy puss!' roared Charley, with flaming face. 'How dare you!'

'There! I knew I was right,' laughed the girl. 'I'm not a bit afraid of you, Charley Vining. But, I say, such a game: there, hold your arms, and I could jump down from here right on to the dear old mare just before you, and you could hold me tight, and we'd play at you being young Lochinvar, and gallop off with me. Wouldn't it be fun?'

'But there's no bridegroom to dandle his bonnet and plume,' laughed Charley.

'There's an ungallant cavalier!' said Nelly, with her wicked eyes dancing with glee. 'Now, if it had been Miss Bed—ha, ha, ha!' she shrieked, as Charley made a dash at her by forcing his mare half-way up the bank. 'Don't you do that, Charley, or you'll go down again, and have to be carried on a gate—and I don't want you to be hurt any more,' she said seriously. 'But there, I must go back and save my poor dear darling Miss Bedford from being bored to death by old stupid. I'm glad I've seen . you, though; it's done me ever so much good. I say, Charley Vining, isn't Miss Bedford nice?'

'I daresay she is; but I know very little of her,' said Charley coolly.

'O, there's a story!' exclaimed down-right Nelly. 'I know you think ever so much of her, or else you would not stop looking miserable after her. There, I've done, and I won't tease you any more; but I do want to borrow sixpence. Old Max wouldn't lend me one if I was starving. Thank you! O, a shilling!' exclaimed Nelly, actively catching the coin he threw. 'Now I'm going; but, I say, do come and see us. You would like my Miss Bedford so!'

Before Charley Vining could answer, Nelly had dashed off, taking a short cut, and he saw her no more; but from that day Charley's spirits rose; and when once or twice more he encountered the walking party, he did not feel so troubled of heart, but rode gaily up, saluting all, taking the first opportunity of frowning and shaking his head at merry laughing Nelly.

CHAPTER XIV.

A FAMILY PARTY.

'SURELY, Miss Bedford, you never think of going to Sir Philip Vining's party such a figure as that!'

It was the day of the Blandfield Court invitation, and the ladies were assembling in the drawing-room. For, some days before, in accordance with his promise, Sir Philip had been over to the Elms, taking Laura quite by surprise when he supplemented his invitation by a request that Miss Bedford might also be of the party.

'Miss Bedford—our governess!' stammered Laura, completely taken aback.

But she was herself again the next instant, as she saw through the arrangement.

'Sir Philip has been deceived,' she thought;
'but I am not so easily put off, nor yet cast
off,' she muttered.

What should she do? Display open
anger, or temporise until Ella Bedford could
be dismissed—ignominiously dismissed—
from her situation?

Laura Bray was angry, and therefore
she talked to herself in strong language,
and called things by unpleasant names.
But she must act in some way, she thought;
it would never do for her to give up all for
which her ambitious nature thirsted. She
had set herself upon being Lady Vining,
and after a fashion she loved Charley, who,
from being free and friendly, and on happy
laughing terms with her, seemed daily to
be growing more and more distant; for
she was not deceived by his assumed socia-
bility. She herself had acted so as to try
and efface the past; but there was still the

recollection of the conservatory scene, and though she tried to set it down as merely a bit of flirtation—one that she ought to pass over without notice—her heart would not accept of the flattering unction ; for she knew Charley Vining to be too sterling, too generous a man to trifle with the feelings of any woman.

Then why was he trifling with her? she exclaimed vehemently. Had she no claims to his consideration? There was a dull heavy feeling came over her, as she thought of how he had never been more than friend to her, and that the warmth had been entirely on one side.

But she felt that it would not do to show her anger—kindness would perhaps work a change ; and until her rival—no, she would not dignify her with that title— till this governess had gone, she would assume an appearance of sorrow, trying the while to win Charley back from his passing fancy. She could have bitten her tongue for the ill-judged hasty words she had spoken; but O, if she could but detect this Miss Bedford in some light coquettish act, some behaviour too frivolous for her position, it should go hard with her!—for at the present—probably on account of the dislike openly shown—Mrs. Bray and her hopeful son seemed disposed to treat their dependent with more consideration, which was really the case on the part of the former, whose mental constitution was such that she could not conceive the possibility of any one holding a paid position to perform certain duties possessing the sensitiveness and thoughts of a lady.

Laura had determined to temporise, and also to counterplot. It struck her that Sir Philip had been deceived, and hurriedly rising, she left the room.

It was evident to her sharpened percep-
tibilities that it was Charley's doing that
Miss Bedford was invited; and she determined Sir Philip Vining should see who was
the lady his son wished to be of the party.

Laura's heart beat quickly, as, with assumed kindness and gentleness of mien, she
returned from the schoolroom with Ella,
and introduced her to Sir Philip.

'I thought that Miss Bedford would
like to thank you herself, Sir Philip, for
your kind invitation,' she said, by way of
explanation of her sudden act; and then
she watched attentively the effect produced.

She was right. Sir Philip was startled,
and as he rose to cordially greet and repeat
his invitation, he gazed almost wonderingly
at the sweet mien and gentle face before
him, raising Ella's hand, and with all the
grace of an old courtier, kissing it respect-
fully, moved by the true homage he felt for

so much youth and beauty. But as he released her hand, there was a troubled puzzled look in the old gentleman's face—a
look that was still there when at last he
took his leave to go thoughtfully homeward; for now it again struck him that
Charley's impressive demand that the governess should be asked was a little strange,
though here was the key.

Sir Philip dismissed the thought that
oppressed him, though. Charley was too
noble to be moved by any disloyal acts;
and as to stooping—pooh! it was absurd!
He was growing an old woman, full of ner-
vous fears and fancies; and casting his
'whimsies,' as he called them, away, he
entered with all his heart into the prepara-
tions for the little fête.

And now the day had arrived, and the
ladies were assembling in the drawing-room,
where Mr. Bray and 'Mr. Maximilian' were

already waiting. Mrs. Bray had sailed and rustled into the room in a tremendously stiff green brocade dress, to be complimented by her lord as resembling a laurel hedge, and by her son for her May-day aspect and Jack-in-the-green look. But Mrs. Bray was satisfied, and that was everything. Her satisfaction was evident by the way in which she swept round the room, making a vortex that caught up the light chairs and loose articles that came within its reach.

'Bai Jove, there, why don't you mind!' exclaimed Max, as the glossy hat left upon the couch was sent spinning across the room. 'Why don't you sit down?'

Mrs. Bray did not reply, but she would not have sat down in that dress, save in the carriage, upon any consideration—at all events, not until after it had been seen at Blandfield.

Max's hat was made smooth sooner than his temper, and he was still muttering and grumbling when Nelly and her sisters came bounding in, like three tall, thin, peripatetic tulips, followed closely by Laura, glorious with black hair, flashing eyes, amber moiré, and black lace.

Mr. Onesimus Bray placed his hands in his pockets and walked smilingly round his daughter, in whom he took immense pride; but the attempt that he made to kiss her was received with a shriek of horror, his daughter darting back beyond his reach, and at the same time bringing forth an oath from her brother's lips, as she swept the glossy, newly-brushed hat from the marqueterie table whereon it had been placed for safety.

'For shame, Max!' exclaimed his mother.

'Bai Jove, then, it's enough to make

an angel swear! How would you like a fellow to tread on your bonnets?'

The ladies shuddered.

'Never mind, then—a poor old Max!' exclaimed mischievous Nelly, who had but a few minutes before been snubbed by her brother; and, stooping down, she picked up the unfortunate hat, and, before she could be arrested, carefully brushed all the nap up the wrong way, Max sitting completely astounded the while at the outrage put upon him.

What he would have said remains to this day unknown. His mouth had gasped open after the fashion of an expiring aquarium pet, and he was about to ejaculate, when he stopped short; for Ella Bedford came quietly into the room, the centre, as it were, of a soft cloud of gray barége, which gave to her pale gentle features almost an ethereal expression, but which

called forth from the gorgeous amber
queen the remark standing at the head of
this chapter:

'Surely, Miss Bedford, you never think
of going to Sir Philip Vining's party such
a figure as that!'

Ella coloured up, and then said gently:

'Shall I change the dress for a plain
muslin, Miss Bray?'

'O, I'm sure I don't know!' exclaimed
Laura, with a toss. 'I think—'

'I think the dress looks uncommonly
nice, Miss Bedford—I do, bai Jove!' drawled
Max, fixing his glass in his eye, and staring
furiously.

It was the first act of kindness Max
Bray had done for many a long day; but it
caused a shrinking sensation in her for
whom it was intended, while Laura darted
at her a fierce look of hatred, and then an
angry glance at her brother.

Ella looked inquiringly at Mrs. Bray, as if for instructions; but that lady always sided with son Max, as did Mr. Bray, as far as he dared, with his daughter.

'I almost think—' he ventured to observe.

'Don't talk stuff, Ness!' shrieked his lady. 'What do you know about a lady's dress? If it was a fleece or a pig— There, I think Miss Bedford's things will do very nicely indeed; and if some people would only dress as neatly, it wouldn't half ruin their parents in dressmakers' bills.'

Laura did not condescend to answer, but throwing herself into a chair, she took up a book, pretending to read, but holding it upside down, till Nelly laughingly called attention to the fact.

'Pert child!' exclaimed Laura fiercely.

'Don't care!' laughed Nelly. 'So the book *was* upside down; and I'd rather be a pert child than a disagreeable, sour old maid!'

'You'd better send that rude tom-boy to bed—you had, bai Jove!' drawled Max.

'Ah!—and I'd rather be a rude tomboy than a great girl, bai Jove, Mr. Max!' cried Nelly; whereupon Mr. Bray laughed, Mrs. Bray scolded, and Nelly pretended to cry, directing a comical look the while at her father, who, whatever his weakness, was passionately fond of his girls.

The crunching of the gravel by the wheels of the wagonette put a stop to the rather unpleasant scene, when, to Laura's surprise, Max jumped up and handed Ella down to the carriage, returning afterwards for his sister, who favoured him with a peculiarly meaning look; one which he replied to in as supercilious a manner as he could assume.

'What does it mean, Max?' she whispered, as they descended the stairs. 'More affection for your little sisters?'

'My dear Laura,' drawled Max, 'will you take my advice and adopt a motto?'

'Motto?' said Laura inquiringly.

'Ya-as, bai Jove! the very one for you —just suited to the occasion: *Laissez-aller*. Do you understand?'

Laura looked at him meaningly, but made no reply, for they had reached the carriage.

CHAPTER XV.

IN spite of her annoyance, Laura's eyes sparkled when they reached the Court; for Sir Philip hurried to the carriage, welcoming the party most warmly, and, handing her out, he led her himself to the beautiful little kiosk, and then took her from place to place, according to her attentions that made more than one match-making mamma with marriageable daughters look meaningly at the same daughters, and then think of Charley Vining with a sigh.

But if Laura was in high glee, so was not Max, who had to stand by while Charley carried off Ella Bedford, Nelly laughingly fastening upon his other arm.

'A rude coarse beast, bai Jove!' muttered Max elegantly, as he tried vainly to get the little button of his glove secured. 'Let him have a fall again, and see if I'll go to his help!'

'I shall come with you if I may,' said Nelly demurely.

'To be sure!' laughed Charley, whose heart throbbed with pleasure as he felt—nay, hardly felt—the light pressure of the gray glove upon his arm. 'Miss Bedford won't mind, I hope. Do you know, Miss Bedford, I'm rather glad you are with us? I'm almost afraid Nelly means some inroad upon my purse.'

'No, I don't,' said Nelly, 'so don't be afraid;' and then she walked very demurely by their side, Charley encouraging her to stay upon observing Ella's constraint and troubled looks.

'She'd be off like a frightened pigeon—

dove, I mean!' muttered Charley, as he looked down at the almost painful face beside him. But a little quiet conversation upon current topics seemed to set her more at ease, and, after awhile, Hugh Lingon approaching, Charley Vining whispered, loudly enough, though, for Nelly to hear:

'Now I'm going, Miss Bedford, for here comes Nelly's intended. I hope you will play the *chaperone* most stringently.'

Nelly rewarded him with a sharp pinch as he left them, Hugh Lingon taking his place; and Ella, whose heart beat almost painfully, asking herself the reason why.

But Charley Vining had laid his plans that day, and he felt he must proceed with caution. So hurrying himself, he acted the part of host with admirable tact, picking out the ladies who seemed neglected, forming sets for croquet, handing refreshments, or escorting little parties to the lake-like

river for boating; distributing himself, as
it were, throughout the grounds, and at last
interrupting a tête-à-tête between Laura
and Hugh Lingon, who had soon forsaken
the ladies left in his charge.

Laura commenced a little *minauderie*,
professing to be unable to leave Mr. Lingon;
but she gave up directly she saw Charley's
laugh, for she knew that it would be—nay,
was—seen through. She knew Charley
Vining to be different from most men of
her acquaintance; and accepting his offer,
she gladly took his arm, making the match-
making mammas to whisper, as the handsome couple passed through the grounds,
' There, didn't I tell you so?' and then to
gossip about how they had had their sus-
picions concerning the purpose of the fête.

But Laura's pleasure was but short-
lived; for though Charley was pleasant,
gay, and chatty, he was nothing more, and

though he carefully avoided referring to the croquet-party, she felt that he was not as she could wish.

'He'll go back to her as soon as, with any decency, he can,' she thought; and her teeth were set, and her fingers clenched, pressing the nails almost through her gloves, as she forced back a sigh.

But she soon cheered up, for she told herself it was not for long, and determined to try if gentleness would gain the day; she listened to all her companion said, striving the while, without being obtrusive, to obliterate her past words of anger.

Laura was wrong; for it was not for a considerable time, and until he had played cavalier to many a lady—winning the thanks and smiles of Sir Philip, who was delighted at his son's efforts — that he sought once more Ella Bedford, followed by Sir Philip's eyes; the old gentleman gazing uneasily after him as he went up and offered his arm, which was reluctantly taken.

'I'm going now,' said Nelly, who had kept with her guard the whole time; 'I want something to eat. I declare, Charley Vining, I've only had one thin slice of butter spread with bread-crumbs, and a cup of tea;' and before a word could be said, she had darted off.

Sir Philip's were not the only eyes that followed Charley Vining to where sat Ella Bedford; for as Max Bray followed him at a distance, as if by accident Laura did the same, and brother and sister gave genuine starts as they encountered at the union of two alleys.

'Grows quite romantic, bai Jove!' sneered Max; but he relapsed into an uncomfortable look on seeing the penetrating gaze directed at him by his sister.

'Let me take your arm,' she said coldly; and then, as the shades of evening were fast falling, they walked slowly on together, towards a part of the grounds now apparently deserted.

Meanwhile Charley Vining had led Ella across the lawn, pressing her to partake of some refreshment, but in vain; and at last, in spite of herself, she found that she was alone with him, in a secluded part of the grounds.

'There is a seat here,' said Charley. 'Shall we rest for a few minutes?'

'It would hardly be advisable,' was the quiet reply; 'the evening is damp.' And then for a few moments there was a pause, as they still walked slowly on, Charley with his heart beating heavily, and Ella eager to return to the throng upon the lawn—a throng that the afternoon through she had avoided—and hardly liking to speak, lest she might betray her agitation, and that she looked upon this otherwise than as an ordinary attention of host to one of his guests.

For Ella was not blind: her woman's instinct had whispered to her respecting the many attentions pressed upon her, and she trembled as she recalled the night when the cross was returned; for her heart told her that such things must not be—that she must be cold and cautious, guarding and steeling herself against tender emotions, for she was but the poor paid governess, and this man, whose arm she lightly touched, was almost engaged to Laura Bray.

But the silence was broken at length by Charley, who spoke deeply, as he stopped short by a standard covered with pale white roses, whose perfume seemed shed around upon the soft night air.

'Miss Bedford,' he said, 'I have been

in pain, almost in agony, for many days
past; and till I found that I had been
wronging you, it seemed to me that life
was going to be unbearable.'

'Pain!—wronging me!' exclaimed Ella.

'Yes,' he said; 'but hear me out. I
am no polished speaker, Miss Bedford—
only a simple, blunt, and I hope honest and
truthful man. A week or two since I believed that you favoured the suit of Max
Bray: to-night I will not insult you with
questions, but tell you honestly I do not
believe that to be the case; and when the
conviction flashed upon me that I was
wrong, I tell you frankly my heart leaped
with joy. You may ask why: I will tell
you.'

'Mr. Vining,' exclaimed Ella, 'this
must not be; you forget yourself, your position—you forget me when you talk so.
Pray lead me back.'

'You speak as if my words pained you, Miss Bedford,' said Charley huskily. 'Pray forgive me if they do. Nay, but a few minutes longer.'

He caught one hand in his, and as she glanced for an instant in his direction, the rising moon gleaming through the trees lit up his handsome earnest face, photographing it, as it were, upon her brain; for to her dying day she never forgot that look—that countenance so imploringly turned upon her.

'Miss Bedford—Ella,' he whispered, 'I love you tenderly and devotedly! This is no light declaration: till I saw you, woman never occupied my thoughts. You see by my brusque ways, my bluntness, that I have been no dallier in drawing-rooms, no holder of lady's silk. Till now, my loves have been in the stables, kennels, fields. Blunt language this—uncomplimentary perhaps;

but I am no courtier. I speak as I feel, and I tell you that to win your love in return would be to make me a happy man.'

'Mr. Vining,' exclaimed Ella, vainly trying to release her hand, 'lead me back, pray!'

'Nay,' said Charley, with sadness in his tones, 'I will not force you to listen to me;' and he released her hand. 'I was hopeful that you would have listened to my suit.'

'Indeed—indeed,' said Ella, 'I cannot, Mr. Vining: it can never be. You forget —position—me!'

She could say no more—her words seemed to stifle her; and had she continued speaking, she felt that she would have burst into tears.

'I forget nothing,' said Charley, almost sternly. 'How can I forget? How can I ever forget? But surely,' he said, once more catching her hand in his—'surely you cannot with that sweet gentle face be cruel, and love to torture one who has spoken simply the truth—laid bare to you his feelings! You believe what I say?'

'Yes, yes!' almost sobbed Ella. 'But indeed—indeed it can never be. Do not think me either harsh or cruel, for I mean it not.'

'What am I to think then?' said Charley bitterly. 'Is it that you reject me utterly, or am I so poor a wooer that you would have me on my knees, protesting, swearing? No; I wrong you again: it is not that,' he exclaimed passionately. 'Look here, Ella'—he plucked one of the white roses, tearing his hand as he did so, the blood appearing in a long mark across the back—'emblematic,' he said, smiling sadly, 'of my love. You see it has its smarts and pains. You refused me so slight a gift once, but take this; and though I am a man I can freely say that my love for you is as pure and spotless as that simple flower. You will not refuse that ?'

He could see the tears in her eyes, and that her face was drawn as if with pain; but one trembling hand was extended to take the flower; then, before he could recover from his surprise, she had turned from him and fled; when, with almost a groan, he threw himself upon the garden-seat, remaining motionless for a few moments, and then rising to hurry back to the marquee.

CHAPTER XVI.

Two minutes had scarcely elapsed before there was the faint rustling of a lady's dress and the creaking of a boot, and then two pale faces—those of brother and sister—appeared from a neighbouring clump of evergreens, gazed cautiously about for a few moments, and then moved away in another direction; the moon just beginning to cast their shadows upon the dewy lawn upon whose turf they walked, perhaps because it hushed their footsteps.

They had hardly disappeared before there was another faint rustling, and, eagerly peering about, Nelly Bray appeared, her girlish face looking half merry, half anxious, in the moonlit glade.

'A nasty, disagreeable, foxy pair of old sneaks!' she exclaimed—'to go peeping and watching about like that, and all because they were as jealous as—as jealous as —well, there, I don't know what. I know I was watching too, but I wouldn't have done so for a moment, if it hadn't been to see what they were going to do. I wouldn't have been so mean and contemptible—that I wouldn't! But O, wasn't it grand!' she exclaimed, clasping her hands. 'Ah, don't I wish I was like Miss Bedford, to have such a nice boy as Charley Vining to fall in love with me and tell me of it, and then for me to reject him like that! I don't believe she meant it, though, that I don't. She couldn't! Nobody could resist Charley Vining: he's ever so much nicer than Hugh Lingon, and I'd run away with him to-morrow, if he asked me—see if I wouldn't! But there ain't no fear of that. I knew he

was in love with her—I was sure of it. And
didn't he speak nicely! Just as if he felt
every word he said, and meant it all—and
he does, too, I know; for he's a regular
trump, Charley is, and I shall say so again,
as there's no one to hear me—he's a regular
trump, that he is; and I don't care what
any one says. Wouldn't it be nice to be
Miss Bedford's bridesmaid! I should wear
—Here's somebody coming!'

Nelly darted off, reaching the door just
as leavetakings were in vogue; Sir Philip
and Charley handing the Bray family to the
waiting carriages; but in spite of their efforts, there was an appearance of constraint
visible.

' Why, here's the little rover!' exclaimed
Charley, as Nelly appeared. ' Where have
you been?'

' Looking after and helping my friends,
as a rover should, Mr. Croquet-player!' ex-

claimed Nelly pertly, as she looked Charley full in the face; while, as he was helping her on with a shawl, she found means to make him start by saying:

'Look out! Max and Laura were listening!'

The next moment the carriage had driven off, leaving Charley standing motionless, and thinking of the pale-faced girl who had leaned so lightly upon his arm as he handed her to the carriage, and wondering what would follow.

'Charley, my dear boy, the Miss Lingons!'

So spoke Sir Philip, rousing the young man from his abstraction, when he hastened to make up for his want of courtesy as guest after guest departed, till the last carriage had ground the gravel of the drive, for the fête was at an end. But as Sir Philip sat alone in his library, thoughtful and fatigued,

it seemed to him that the affair had not
been so successful as he could have wished;
and that night—ay, and for many nights to
come—he was haunted by a vision of a fair-
haired girl, with soft gray eyes which
seemed to ask the protection of all on
whom they rested; and somehow Sir Philip
Vining sighed, for he felt troubled, and
that matters were not going as he had intended.

Meanwhile the Brays' wagonette rolled
on till it reached the Elms. Hardly a
word had been spoken on the return journey; for Mr. Bray was hungry, Mrs. Bray
cross, and Max and his sister thoughtful,
as was Ella Bedford. Nelly had spoken
twice, but only to be snubbed into silence;
and it was with a feeling of relief shared
by all, that they descended and entered
the house.

Mrs. Bray and her lord directly took

chamber candlesticks, Mr. Bray whispering
something to the butler respecting a tray
and dressing-room. Ella hurried away
with her charges, while Max opened the
drawing-room door and motioned to his
sister to enter; but she took no heed of his
sign, as, with angry glances, she followed
Ella till she had disappeared.

'Come here,' said Max. 'I want you.'

'I'm tired,' said Laura. 'You must
keep it till the morning.'

'I tell you I want you now!' he exclaimed almost savagely, the man's real
nature flashing out as he cast the thin veil
of society habit aside, and spoke eagerly.

'Then I shall not come,' said Laura,
turning away.

'If you dare to say a word about all
this, I'll never forgive you!' he whispered.

'I can live without Mr. Max Bray's for-
giveness,' said Laura tauntingly.

'Confound you, come down!' he exclaimed, as Laura ascended the stairs.   'I
will not have her spoken to about it unless
I speak.'

'Good-night, Max,' was the cool reply;
and he saw her pass through the swing
door at the end of Mr. Bray's picture-gal-
lery; while foaming and apparently enraged,
he made a bound up a few stairs, but only
to descend again, enter the drawing-room,
and close the door.

The door had hardly closed before
Laura appeared again, without a chamber
candlestick, to lean over the balustrade
eager and listening as she peered down into
the hall.   But there was not a sound to be
heard; and hurrying back along the gallery,
she stopped at Ella's door, and then, without knocking, turned the handle and entered.

CHAPTER XVII.

A VIAL OF WRATH.

'AND, pray, what are you doing here?' exclaimed Laura Bray, as she saw the tall slim form of her sister Nelly standing between her and the object of her dislike.

'Talking to Miss Bedford, if you must know, my dear sister,' said Nelly pertly; but the next moment she encountered a glance from Ella, in obedience to which she was instantly silent; and, crossing over, she kissed the pale girl lovingly, and said, 'Good-night.'

But all this was not lost upon Laura, who bit her lips till Nelly had half hesitatingly quitted the room.

'What sweet obedience!' she then said sarcastically. 'Really, Miss Bedford, you must give me some lessons in the art of winning people's affections. I have no doubt that papa will satisfy you if there is any extra charge.'

Ella did not speak; but her gentle look might have disarmed animosity, as she turned her soft eyes almost appealingly towards her irate visitor. She was in some degree, though, prepared for what was coming, for Nelly had lingered behind to place her on her guard; and as she stood facing Laura she did not shrink, neither did she make answer to the taunts conveyed in those bitter words.

'I trust that you have enjoyed a pleasant evening, Miss Bedford,' continued Laura, who seemed to be working herself up, and gathering together the battalions of her wrath, ready for the storm she meant to thunder upon the defenceless head before her. But still there was no reply in words—nothing but the calm pleading gaze from the soft gray eyes.

'Can we make arrangements for you to be introduced to some other family, where you can carry on your intrigues?'

Still no answer—only a pitiful, almost imploring look that ought to have disarmed the most wrathful. But at this moment Ella involuntarily raised a white rose, which till then had remained concealed, as her hand hung down amidst the soft folds of her dress; and no sooner did Laura catch sight of the blossom than, interpreting the act to be one of insolent triumph, she threw herself upon the shrinking girl, tore the flower from her hand, and flung it upon the floor, where she crushed it beneath her foot as she stamped upon it furiously.

'How dare you!' she almost shrieked,

in tones that bade fair some day to rival
those of Mamma Bray. 'Such cowardly—
such insolent acts! To dare to insult me
after practising your low cunning to-day,
laying your snares for my poor unworldly
brother, and then setting other traps—to—
to—inveigle—to entrap—There, don't look
at me with that triumphant leer! You shall
be turned out of this house, into which you
have gained entrance by false pretences, so as
to act the part of a scheming adventuress!'

For a few moments Laura seemed as if
she would strike the object of her resent-
ment, so fierce was the burst of passion that
came pouring forth—the unlucky act having roused every bitter and angry feeling
in her breast: disappointed love, ambition,
hatred—all were mingled into a poison that
was like venom to her barbed and stinging
words, as she stooped even to abusing the
innocent cause of her dislike.

At length Ella raised her hands, and
spoke deprecatingly; but each appeal only
seemed to rouse Laura to fresh outbursts
of violence, so that at last the bitter taunts
and revilings were suffered in silence, the
angry woman's voice rising louder with her
victim's patience, till, alarmed by her daughter's angry, hysterical cries, Mrs. Bray hurried into the room.

'What is the meaning of all this?' she
shrieked. 'Laura!—Miss Bedford! Are
you both mad?'

Ella was about to speak, but Laura
fiercely interrupted her.

'Speak a word if you dare!' she said.
'I will not have anything said! Such in-
solence is insupportable.'

'But what has Miss Bedford been doing?' shrieked Mrs. Bray. 'You are alarm-
ing the whole house. What does it mean?'

'Nothing. Let it rest,' cried Laura,

cooling down rapidly, but with face a-
flame; for she could not bear her mother
to be a witness to her humiliation, there
being, based on Laura's slight exaggerations
of one or two attentions, a full belief in
the Bray family that even if the question
had not been put by Charley Vining, matters had so far progressed that he was sure
to be her husband: hence her objection to
a word being uttered; and, shrinking back,
Ella stood with bended head, while a passage of arms took place between mother and
daughter, Mrs. Bray's curiosity increasing
with Laura's reticence.

Finding though, at last, that nothing
was to be gained, Mrs. Bray followed Laura
from the room; and Ella, trembling with
excitement and the agitation of many painful hours, was about to welcome the solitude hers at last, when once more the door
opened, and, pale and wild-looking, so that

she felt to pity her, Laura again appeared, closing the door carefully behind her, and then standing to gaze thoughtfully in Ella's face.

She had come to threaten—to try and enforce silence ; but her voice was husky ; the fierce passion which had before sustained her had now passed away, and the weak woman, cut to the heart by disappointment, was once more asserting herself.

For quite five minutes she stood with heaving breast, trying to speak, but the words would not come; and at last, dreading to let the woman she hated and despised, one whom she looked upon as full of deceit and guile, gaze upon and triumph in her tears, Laura turned and fled from the room; and once more Ella was alone.

CHAPTER XVIII.

ANALYSIS OF THE HEART.

ALONE—alone once more in her bedroom, the scene of so many bitter tears, Ella stood with flushed cheeks, and eyes that seemed to burn, thinking of the words that had been uttered to her that day. She held the crushed rose in her hand—the flower Laura had with cruel hand snatched away and cast down, and upon which she had trampled with as little remorse as upon her feelings. But the agitated girl had once more secured the torn blossom, to stand gazing down upon its bruised petals.

What did he say? That he loved her —her whom he had seen so few times! He loved her : he, the heir to a baronetcy, loved her—a poor governess, the persecuted, despised dependent of this family—that his love for her was as pure as that white blossom! It could not be. And yet he had spoken so earnestly; his voice trembled, and those low soft utterances so tenderly, so feelingly whispered, so full of appeal and reverence, were evidently genuine. They were not the words of the thoughtless, the lovers of conquest, the distributors of vain compliments, empty nothings, to every woman who was the toy of the hour. And he was no weak boy, ready to be led away by a fresh face—no empty-headed coxcomb, but a man of sterling worth.

There was a plain, straightforward, manly simplicity in what he had said that went home to her heart; there was a nobility in his disappointment and anger which made her thrill with the awakening of new thoughts, new senses, that had before lain dormant in her breast; there was the sterling ring of the true gentleman in his every act and look and word, and— Ah, but—no—no—no! She was mad to harbour such thoughts, even for an instant; it was folly—all folly. How could she accept him, even if her heart leaned that way? It would be doing him a grievous wrong, blighting his prospects, tying him down to one unworthy of his regard. She could not —she did not love him. Love! What was it to love? She had loved those who were no more; but love him, a stranger! What was it to love?

Beat, beat!—beat, beat!—beat, beat! Heavy throbbings of her poor wounded heart answering the question she had asked, plainly, and in a way that would not be ignored, even though she pressed that flower-burdened hand tightly over the place, and laid the other upon her hot and tingling cheeks. But even if she knew it, could she own to it? No! impossible; not even to herself. That was a secret she could not ponder on, even for an instant.

And yet he had said that he loved her! What were his words? She must recall them once more: that his love for her was as truthful and as pure as that flower— that poor crushed rose.

As she thought on, flushed and trembling, she raised the flower nearer and nearer to her face, gazing at the bruised petals, crushed, torn, and disfigured. It was to her as the reading of a prophecy —that his pure love for her was to become torn and sullied, and that, for her sake, he was to suffer bitter anguish, till, like that flower, his love should wither away. But there would still be the recollection of the sweet words, even as there stayed in the crushed blossom its own sweet perfume, the incense-breathing fragrance, as she raised it more and more till the hot tears began to fall.

No, she did not love him—she could not love him: it was folly—all a dream from which she was awaking; for she knew the end—she knew her days at the Elms must be but few—that, like a discarded servant, she must go : whither she knew not, only that it must be far away—somewhere to dream no more, neither to be persecuted for what she could not help.

No; she did not love him, and he would soon forget her. It could be but a passing fancy. But she esteemed him—she must own to a deep feeling of esteem for one of so noble, frank, and generous a nature. Had he not always been kind and gentle and sympathising—displaying his liking for her with a gentlemanly respect that had won upon her more and more? Yes, she

esteemed him too well, she was too grateful, to injure him ever so slightly; and her
greatest act of kindness would be to hurry
away.

The fragrance from the poor crushed
flower still rose, breathing, as it were, such
love and sweetness; recalling, too, the words
with which it was given so vividly, that, be-
trayed beyond her strength to control the
act, for one brief instant Ella's lips were
pressed softly, lovingly, upon the flower—
petals kissing petals—the bright bee-stung
and ruddy touching the pale and crushed;
and then, firmly and slowly, though each
act seemed to send a pang through her
throbbing heart, Ella plucked the rose in
pieces, telling herself that she was tearing
forth the mad passion as she went on showering down the creamy leaflets, raining
upon them her tears the while, till the bare
stalk alone remained in her hands—her

cruel hands; for had she not been tearing
and rending her own poor breast as every
petal was plucked from its hold? For what
availed the deceit? The time had been
short — they had met but seldom: but
what of that? The secret would burst forth,
would assert itself; and she knew that she
loved him dearly—loved him so that she
would give her life for his sake; and that
to have been his slave—to have been but
near him—to listen to his voice—to see his
broad white forehead, his sun-tinged cheeks,
and clustering brown hair; not to be called
his, but only to be near him—would be life
to her; while to go far—far—far away,
where she might never see him more, would
be, as it were, tottering even into her grave.

No; there was no one looking: it was
close upon midnight, but she glanced guiltily
round, as with burning cheeks she sank
upon her knees, whispering to that wild

beating heart that it could not be wrong. And then she began to slowly gather those petals, taking them up softly one by one, to treasure somewhere—to gaze upon, perhaps, sometimes in secret; for was it not his gift that she had cast down as if it had been naught? She might surely treasure them up to keep in remembrance of what might have been, had hers been a happier lot.

Then came once more the thoughts of the past evening, and more than ever she felt that she must go. She would see him no more, and he would soon forget it all. But would she forget? A sob was the answer — a wild hysterical sob — as she felt that she could not.

One by one, one by one, she gathered those leaflets up to kiss them once again; and that night, flush-cheeked and fevered, she slept with the fragments of the blos-

som pressed tightly to her aching breast,
till calm came with the earliest dawn, and
with the lightening sky dreams of hope and
love and happiness to come, with brighter
days and loving friends, and all joyous and
blissful. She was walking where white-
rose petals showered down to carpet the
earth; the air was sweet with their fragrance, and she was leaning upon his stout
arm as he whispered to her of a love truthful and pure as the flowers around; and
then she awoke to the bare chill of her own
stiffly-papered, poorly-furnished room, as
seen in the gray dawn of a pouring wet
morning, with the wind howling dismally
in the great old-fashioned chimney, the rain
pattering loudly against the window-panes,
and hanging in great trembling beads from
the sash. It was a fit morning, on the
whole, to raise the spirits of one who was
dejected, spiritless, almost heart-broken;

and it was no wonder that Ella Bedford's head sank once more upon the pillow, which soon became wet with her bitter tears.

For how could she meet the different members of that family? She felt as if she was guilty; and yet what had she done? It was not of her seeking. She could have wept again and again in the despair and bitterness of her heart; but her eyes were dried now, and she began to ponder over the scenes of the past night.

She rose at last to go down to the schoolroom, for it was fast approaching eight, and as she descended, her mind was made up as to her future proceedings. She would go carefully on with her duties; but in the course of the morning, if not sent for sooner, she would herself seek Mrs. Bray, and ask to be set at liberty, so that she might elsewhere seek a home—one that should afford her rest and peace.

CHAPTER XIX.

BREAKFAST over at the Elms, and no improvement in the weather. Maximilian Bray said that it was impossible to go out, 'bai Jove!' so he was seated in a low *bergère* chair in the drawing-room. He had taken a book from a side table as if with the intention of reading; but it had fallen upon the floor, Max Bray not being at the best of times a reading man; and now he was busy at work plotting and planning with a devotion worthy of a better cause. His head was imparting some of its ambrosia to the light chintz chair-cover, for he had impatiently thrown the antimacassar under the table. Then he

fidgeted about a little, altered the sit of his
collar and wristbands, and at last, as if not
satisfied with his position, he removed his
chair farther into the bay, so that the light
drapery of the flowing curtains concealed
his noble form from the view of any one
entering the room, when, apparently satisfied, he gazed thoughtfully through the
panes at the soaked landscape.

Max Bray had not been long settled to
his satisfaction when Laura entered, shutting the door with a force that whispered—
nay, shouted—of a temper soured by some
recent disappointment. She gave a sharp
glance round the room, and then, seeing
no one, threw herself into a chair, a sob
at the same moment bursting from her
breast.

'She shall go — that she shall!' exclaimed Laura suddenly, as she gave utterance to her thoughts. 'Such deceit!—such

quiet carneying ways! But there shall be no more of it: she shall go!'

Laura Bray ceased speaking; and, starting up, she began to pace the room, but only to stop short on seeing her brother gazing at her with a half-mocking, half-amused expression of countenance from behind the curtain.

' You here, Max!' she exclaimed, colouring hotly.

' Bai Jove, ya-a-as!' he drawled. 'But, I say, isn't it a bad plan to go about the house shouting so that every one can hear your bewailings, because a horsey cad of a fellow gives roses to one lady and thorns to another?'

' What *do* you mean, Max?' said Laura.

' What do I mean! Well, that's cool, bai Jove! O, of course nothing about meetings by moonlight alone, and roses and vows, and that sort of spooneyism!

But didn't you come tearing and raving in here, saying that she should go, and that you wouldn't stand it, and swore—'

'O, Max!' cried Laura passionately.

'Bai Jove! why don't you let a fellow finish?' drawled Max. 'Swore, I said—swore like a cat just going to scratch; and I suppose that you would like to scratch, eh?'

'But, Max, did you really hear what I said?' cried Laura.

'Hear? Bai Jove! of course I did—every word. Couldn't help it. Good job it was only me.'

'How could you be so unmanly as to listen!' cried Laura.

'Listen? Bai Jove, how you do talk! I didn't listen; you came and raved it all at me. And so she shall go, shall she?'

'Yes!' exclaimed Laura, firing up, and speaking viciously, 'that she shall—a deceitful creature! I see through all her plots and plans, and I'll—'

'Tear her eyes out, won't you, my dear, eh? Now just look here, Laury: you think me slow, and all that sort of fun, and that I don't see things; but I'm not blind. So the big boy has kicked off his allegiance, has he? and run mad after the little governess, has he? and the big sister is very angry and jealous!'

'Jealous, indeed!' cried Laura—'and of a creature like that!'

'All right; only don't interrupt,' said Max mockingly. 'Jealous, I said, and won't put up with it, and quite right too! But, all the same, I'm not going to have her sent away.'

'And why not, pray?' cried Laura with flashing eyes.

'Because I don't choose that she shall go,' said Max coolly.

Laura started, and then in silence brother and sister sat for a few moments gazing in each other's eyes, a flood of thought sweeping the while across the brain of the latter as she recalled a score of little things till then unnoticed, or merely attributed to a natural desire to flirt; but, with the key supplied by Max Bray's last words, Laura felt that she could read him with ease, and her brow contracted as she tried to make him shrink; but that did not lie in her power.

'Max!' she exclaimed at last, 'I'm ashamed of you! It's mean, and contemptible, and base, and grovelling! I'm disgusted! Why, you'll be turning your eyes next to the servants' hall!'

'Thank you, my dear!' drawled Max. 'Very high-flown and grand! But I shall be content at present with the schoolroom. And now suppose I say I'm ashamed of you; and, bai Jove, I am! A girl of your style and pretensions, instead of winking at what you've seen, or coming to your brother for counsel, to go howling about the house—'

'Max!' half shrieked Laura.

'I don't care—bai Jove, I don't!' he exclaimed. 'So you do go howling about the house like a forlorn shepherdess, bai Jove, so that every one can see what a fool you are making of yourself!'

'And pray what would my noble brother's advice be?' cried Laura sarcastically.

Max Bray was another man for an instant, as, starting up in his chair, he caught his sister by the arm, drawing her towards him until she sank down in a sitting position upon the ottoman at his feet, when, with the drawling manner and affectation gone, he leaned over her, talking in a low earnest voice, and so impressively, that

Laura's mocking smile gave place to a look of intense interest. She drew nearer to him at length, as he still talked on eagerly; then she clasped her hands together, and rested them upon his knees.

'But no!' she exclaimed, suddenly starting as it were from something which seemed to enthral her, 'I will not be a party to it, Max!'

'Very good, my dear,' he said cavalierly; 'then you shall have the pleasure of watching progress, and seeing yourself thrust out, if you please. Bai Jove, though, Laury, I did think you were a girl of more spirit! Seems really, though, a good deal smitten, does Charley.'

Laura's countenance changed, and her teeth were set together.

'I shall let him go on, then, for my part, if you choose it to be so.'

'I choose!' cried Laura, with the tears

in her eyes. 'O, Max, why do you torture
me?'

'Then look here!' said Max.

And once more he leaned over towards
her, assuming a quiet ease, but at the same
time it was plain to see that he was greatly
excited. He talked on and on impressively,
with the effect of making Laura's lips part
and her eyes to glisten with a strange light.
Then a pallor overspread her countenance,
but only to be swept away by a look of
exultation as Max still talked on.

'But it is impossible, Max!' cried Laura,
at length.

'Perhaps you'll leave me to judge about
that, and think only of your own part!' he
said coolly. 'Is my advice—are my offers
—worth accepting?'

'O yes, Max, yes!' cried Laura excitedly; 'I'd do anything!'

'I don't want you to do anything,' said

Max, smiling with triumph; 'only what I advise. Help me, and I will help you with all my heart. But I always knew that you would. You say that you don't like my choice. Well and good ; I might say that I don't like yours. Perhaps my affair will come to nothing ; but, anyhow, you are the gainer. I won't say anything about hating, but let you have your selection. Now let me have mine. But if you have anything better to propose, I am ready to listen.'

'But I have no plans, Max. I only thought of her being sent away ; I'm half broken-hearted and worn-out with disappointment !'

'Yes, just so. I expected as much, and I was waiting here to see you,' said Max. 'I'm not blind, Laury, nor deaf either. I heard you two shouting across the hall. So you've been telling the old lady that some one shall go, have you ?'

'Yes, I have!' exclaimed Laura, ignoring the past conversation; 'and she shall go too! Mamma did promise me.'

'Ya-a-as, I know,' said Max, relapsing into his drawl; 'but that was before she promised me. The second will counts before the first made. But, as I said before, and we understand now, she's not going—so there's an end of it.'

'O, of course!' cried Laura passionately. 'Everything must be as mamma's dear boy wishes! He shall have everything he likes, and do as he likes, and say what he likes, and every one else is to give way to him!'

'Bai Jove, now, don't be an idiot!' exclaimed Max. 'What's the good—now that I'm working on your side, and we have got to understand one another—of running back like this? I'm obliged to speak plain, and to tell you that you are only a stupid child, Laury, and that you've taken a liking for

another stupid child—and there's a pair of
you; but all the same, if you do as I tell
you, all will come right!'

Laura tossed her head, and seemed
somewhat mollified, perhaps from being
reminded of her folly.

'There,' said Max, 'that will do for this
morning; so now do just as I tell you, and
leave all the rest to me. But is it a bargain?'

Laura Bray was thoughtful for a few
minutes. She was placed in a position
which required consideration: the languid
brother, whom she had hitherto almost despised, was asking her to forego one purpose
for the sake of an equivalent; but it was
the fact of his asking her to trust herself
entirely to his guidance that troubled her;
and for a while she shrank from yielding.

'Well,' he said again, 'is it a bargain?'

Still Laura did not answer, but re-

mained gazing fixedly at the speaker, who
watched her as attentively, his flushed check
and eager eyes displaying the interest he
took in the affair. At last, though, she
leaned forward, and taking one of his arms
between her hands,

'I never trusted you yet, Max,' she
said.

'Sisterly, very—but perfectly true,' he
exclaimed, laughing.

'But I will, Max, this time. But if
you play me false—'

'Hush!' ejaculated Max, throwing himself back in his chair, and forcing his glass
beneath his brow to stare at the new-comer;
for at that moment the drawing-room door
opened, and Ella Bedford stood upon the
threshold.

CHAPTER XX.

'I BEG pardon,' said Ella, upon seeing who occupied the room. 'I thought that Mrs. Bray would be here.'

'No, not here now, Miss Bedford,' said Max, in his best style. 'But take a chair; she won't be long first. Don't run away, Laury.'

'I must; I have a letter or two to write,' said Laura, trying hard to appear calm, and play into her brother's hand. But so far the efforts of brother and sister were without effect; for, with a few words of thanks, Ella withdrew; and a minute after the tones of Mrs. Bray's voice were heard in loud expostulation, and coming nearer and nearer, till the door was flung open, and she entered, literally driving Ella before her.

'There, only think, Maximilian dear,' shrieked Mrs. Bray; 'here's Miss Bedford been to say she must go!'

'Quite out of the question,' said Max. 'Bai Jove, what can you be thinking of, Miss Bedford? Why, poor Nelly would break her heart.'

Ella started slightly, for Max Bray had touched a tender chord, and she remained silent, with the tears standing in her eyes, as the form of Nelly forced itself upon her imagination.

'It would be so inconvenient,' shrieked Mrs. Bray; 'and you suit us so very well. I was only yesterday saying to your master—I mean, to Mr. Bray—that the way in which those children have improved is perfectly wonderful.'

'Perhaps Miss Bedford will reconsider her sudden determination,' said Laura, in a voice which trembled with the struggle she had with self to obey the intelligent look darted at her by her brother.

'I have quietly thought it over,' said Ella, looking with wondering eyes at the last speaker, as she felt unable to comprehend this sudden change, 'and it is really absolutely necessary that I should leave.'

'I'm sure you never will with my consent,' shrieked Mrs. Bray. 'I think you a very nice young person indeed, Miss Bedford; and even Mr. Maximilian made the remark this very morning, how pleased he was with the way in which you manage the children. And really, Miss Bedford, if it is a matter of two pounds more in your wages, I'm sure Mr. Bray won't object to raising you. It's so troublesome to have

to change, you see. But now that you are
aware how much we are disposed to keep
you, I think you will alter your mind.'

'Indeed, madam—' cried Ella.

'There, there, there — pray don't be
hasty!' shrieked Mrs. Bray. 'That's what
I always say to the servants: "Don't do
anything without plenty of consideration."
You are young yet, Miss Bedford, and have
not yet learned how much easier it is to
lose than to gain a situation. Now take
my advice, and go and think it over. No,
I won't hear another word now; only remember this: I wish you to stay, and so
does Mr. Maximilian, who takes great interest in the studies of his sisters, as well
as in their welfare, as you must have found
out before now.'

'Bai Jove, yes!' murmured Max, un-
abashed by the sharp glance sent flashing
at him by his sister.

'I'm afraid,' said Laura with an effort, 'that it is all due to my hasty words, spoken in anger last night. I'm sure I beg your pardon, Miss Bedford: I'm afraid I was in error—labouring under a mistake— been deceived—' She hesitated here as for an instant she encountered Ella's candid, wondering look; but feeling reassured by the thought that Ella did not know how she had played the spy, Laura plucked up courage, and joined with Mrs. Bray in requesting that Ella would quietly reconsider the matter, playing the hypocrite admirably, and little thinking how those soft eyes read the deceit.

'I quite agree with mamma, that you had better calmly think the matter over,' said Laura after a pause.

'Bai Jove, yes!' said Max, rising and going to the door. 'There, I'll leave you all to talk it over.' And, with a parting

glance at Ella, he left the room; but no
sooner was the door closed than Ella started
again, for Max was heard loudly calling,
' Nelly! Nelly!' Then there was the noise
of a scuffle, a smart slap, and two or three
' I won't's!' and ' I sha'n't's!' in the midst of
which Max returned, dragging in Nelly,
very hot and wild-looking; for her conscience told her that she was to be taken
to task for listening amongst the shrubs
the night before.

' There!' said Max, ' I've got another
voter, bai Jove, Miss Bedford! Here, Nelly,
Miss Bedford says she wants to go away
from the Elms; it won't do—'

' What!' cried Nelly, her eyes flashing
as she darted to Ella's side.

' You should say, " I beg your pardon,"
or " I did not catch your words," my dear,'
shrieked Mrs. Bray—' not " what!" '

' Miss Bedford wants to go!' cried Nelly,

not heeding Mamma Bray's words. 'Then you and Laury have done it between you, and it is cruel and wicked, and—and— shameful, and—and beastly—that it is!' cried Nelly, bursting out into a passion of weeping. 'But if she is sent away, I'll run away too, and never come back any more.'

'But, bai Jove! we want her to stop,' cried Max, 'don't you see?'

'Then she will stop,' cried Nelly; 'won't you, Miss Bedford?'

'There, I'm off; I see you womenkind will settle it amongst you,' said Max; and, satisfied that what had threatened to be a check to his plans had been most likely averted, he left the room and sought the solace of a cigar.

END OF VOL. I.

LONDON : ROBSON AND SONS, PRINTERS, PANCRAS ROAD, N.W.